"I want to give you what you need, Zach," Candy said softly.

"You want to give me something, heat me up a glass of milk," he said, his dry, husky laugh rumbling in the dark room.

"Are you always this cautious, Zach?"

He tried to be. That bad things happened when you least expected them was a given in his life. That good things could happen the same way was harder to accept. "I'm not saying no."

She laughed. "You're not saying yes either."

He said nothing, and she got skittish. "I'm sorry, I've made a fool of myself and made you uncomfortable."

"Do I look uncomfortable?" He made room for her on the sofa. "Come on, I won't bite."

She didn't move.

"Unless you want me to." He winked.

She was quiet for a moment. Then he asked, "Why me?"

She smiled and let her fingers brush his hair off his forehead. "Would you believe me if I said you were a good man and you deserve all the love you haven't been getting?"

He watched her, thinking she was going to change her mind. Then he looked into her black eyes and knew. Any woman brave enough to lay it on the line deserved the best he could give. He pressed his lips to hers, and lightning struck. . . .

WHAT ARE *LOVESWEPT* ROMANCES?

They are stories of true romance and touching emotion. We believe those two very important ingredients are constants in our highly sensual and very believable stories in the *LOVESWEPT* line. Our goal is to give you, the reader, stories of consistently high quality that may sometimes make you laugh, sometimes make you cry, but are always fresh and creative and contain many delightful surprises within their pages.

Most romance fans read an enormous number of books. Those they truly love, they keep. Others may be traded with friends and soon forgotten. We hope that each *LOVESWEPT* romance will be a treasure—a "keeper." We will always try to publish

LOVE STORIES YOU'LL NEVER FORGET
BY AUTHORS YOU'LL ALWAYS REMEMBER

The Editors

Loveswept ®568

Terry Lawrence
Dangerous in the Dark

BANTAM BOOKS

NEW YORK · TORONTO · LONDON · SYDNEY · AUCKLAND

DANGEROUS IN THE DARK
A Bantam Book / September 1992

If you would be interested in receiving protective vinyl
covers for your Loveswept books, please write to this address
for information:

Loveswept
Bantam Books
P.O. Box 985
Hicksville, NY 11802

ISBN 0-553-44189-2

Published simultaneously in the United States and Canada

PRINTED IN THE UNITED STATES OF AMERICA

OPM   0 9 8 7 6 5 4 3 2 1

*Dedicated to the men and women
of Cherryland Electric Co-op,
the people who keep the lights on.*

One

Zach Young swung the large yellow line truck into the yard. His plan to take a shortcut home had backfired, the plank bridge over Commencement Creek washed out by the storm. He was four miles from his parents' house as the crow flew, but crows didn't fly in weather like this, he thought. Tiny hail battered his windshield like so much rice thrown at a giant's wedding. An angry giant.

"Buddy, you're zoning out but good," he said out loud.

He had to get some sleep. It didn't matter where, just as long as he got it. He'd been working eighteen-hour days since the series of storms had swept across the prairie in the middle of the week. His supervisor's order that he take six hours paid rest made more sense by the minute. He was beat. Thanks to that swollen river his day would end at Backbridge Farm.

He'd heard someone had bought the place after the last owners had let it sit empty for a year. Rumor had it the new owner was some New York woman looking for a tax dodge. From the looks of it she hadn't moved in yet. Who would it hurt if he camped out on her floor?

Grabbing a blanket from behind his seat, he ran for the back porch. The air smelled of sulfur; lightning had struck nearby. Waiting for the fitful illumination, Zach scanned the silhouetted outline of the barns. No sparks or flames. Probably a tree down. He'd look around tomorrow.

He put his shoulder to the backdoor and gave the handle a rattle, swearing softly under his breath when it didn't budge. "Five and a half hours' sleep," he said with a groan, "is that too much to ask?" The god of thunder replied with a rumbling chuckle.

At six feet Zach didn't relish curling up in his cab any more than he enjoyed breaking into abandoned farmhouses. He stalked back to his truck, ignoring the pounding rain. Slamming the truck door, he radioed in to the office. "Esther, give me a wake-up call in the morning, sweetheart. I'm camping in my cab."

"Will do."

He signed off, impressed as usual at the good-natured way the office staff kept everyone going during a crisis. Esther and Carol must've had four hundred outage calls in the last three days, and they still sounded perky. He smiled and winced. Even his cheekbones were tired. Pulling the blanket around his shoulders, he hiked his heels onto the dash. He'd regret that impromptu shower when the temperature dropped. Under the circumstances, a good blood-warming dream was in order. . . .

"Hello!"

The knock on the window made him jump so high, he thumped his head against the roof as his heels thudded to the floor.

"Are you from the electric company?"

As he rolled down the window his face was pelted by stinging rain. "Who in Sam Hill are you?"

"Candace—" Thunder drowned out the second half. "My power's out."

"Yours and several thousand others', ma'am." From what he could see in the flickering light of the lantern she carried, she was more a miss than a ma'am. "Did you call it in?"

"The phone's out, too. Aren't you here to repair it?"

The question of what exactly he was doing there could only be answered with the words *preparing to sleep on the job.* "I'll call it in. You get out of the rain." He switched on his radio, grimly smiling at the choice words Jack'd have for him when he found out Zach was still working. He couldn't help it, it wasn't in him to sit still when someone was in trouble.

According to Esther and the electric co-op computers, new member Candace Wharton shared a line with three other houses. But three houses didn't count for much when whole substations were blown.

Zach hopped down from his truck, every bone and muscle protesting, and trudged toward the small square of light inside the backdoor. "Zach Young," he introduced himself, "Prairieland Electric Co-op." He explained the outage situation until his voice grated to a stop. He was so tired, he wasn't even sure he'd been coherent. *They'd get the power on as soon as they could. They had crews working around the clock. . . .*

She nodded, looking up at him as if he were her personal knight in armor come to make the lights go on. Her eyes were bright black, the pupils swallowing up whatever color they'd normally have. The lantern flame shimmered a low welcoming gold on the kitchen table.

"If we get some extra crews, you ought to be out no

more than two or three days," he repeated, bracing himself.

She didn't argue, didn't wail about what she'd do until then, didn't complain about meat thawing in her freezer. She just nodded some more and peered up at him.

"Mrs. Griddell is just down the road, she can put you up if you—"

"Oh no." She shook her head, straight black hair wavering back and forth, level with her chin. A pink headband held it in place, all except spiky wet bangs brushing the tops of her eyebrows. "I can manage fine. What about you?" Her tentative smile revealed perfect white teeth, lips rosy in contrast, and caring, lots of caring.

Zach shook his head, and the room spun slightly. He set a hand on a ladderback kitchen chair and tried not to topple over. "I'll be heading home."

Getting to his parents' from there would mean twelve slow-going miles the long way around, but he'd risk it. Hallucinations about ministering angels in abandoned farmhouses weren't pretty. She sure was. "You might have to rough it, but you'll be fine once the sun comes up."

"Don't go," she said suddenly. "I mean, not without some coffee. It'll wake you up for the drive. It's a terrible night to be out."

Because it would take more effort than he could spare to talk her out of it, he sat down. The chair squeaked under his weight. Tiredness crept up his legs until he felt like the Tin Man, rusting in place. His chin dipped toward his chest for support. To keep his eyes focused, he fumbled with the wick adjuster on the camping lantern. The stem turned, gritty and scratchy, reminding him of his eyelids. Finally the light burned up brighter.

"Oh!" she said, turning from the stove. She smiled at him as if he'd invented fire. "That's wonderful!"

"Is this all the light you've got?"

"I have some candles—still packed somewhere."

"You don't mind the dark?"

"I hate it," she said passionately. "If God had meant us to live in the dark, he wouldn't have put little lights in refrigerators."

He laughed. She was a city girl all right.

She'd slipped on an apron—yellow chicks and blue hens. That didn't countrify her white silk blouse. Not even the jeans hugging her behind could take away the impression of sleek elegance. "You been living here long?" he asked.

"A week. I'm still sorting out the inventory in the outbuildings. The people who owned this—did you know them?"

If he had, he couldn't think of their names now.

"Harkers," she filled in. "They used to sell organically raised vegetables to a restaurant in New York that a friend of mine owns, the Good Earth. After the Harkers closed up shop, Naomi, my friend, complained for a whole year that she couldn't find produce as perfect."

Candy knew he wasn't listening. The rings under the man's eyes were so dark, he looked bruised. Lines ran deep around the edges of his face, like a crumpled piece of brown wrapping paper. She knew if she didn't keep the words rolling, he'd feel obligated to make conversation. So she rattled on, warming to the feeling of having someone to talk to.

"When my divorce came through, I thought of this farm and decided I'd make a go of it. I know I have a ready market in New York with Naomi, and I've always loved gardening."

"Gardening isn't farming."

"Pardon?"

He scowled and seemed to notice for the first time the coffee cup between his hands. He downed the black brew in a gulp. "Hard work, farming."

"I'm a hardy girl."

He'd been trying for a coon's age not to notice. The lamplight had her filtering in and out of his sight along the dim edges of the room. She wasn't overly tall, but she exuded a capable two-feet-on-the-ground attitude. The kind of woman who made a man feel comfortable, not overprotective—until he recalled the way she'd looked up at him outside.

"Why *are* you here?" she'd asked.

Hell if he knew. "Why don't you sit down a minute," he said, suddenly out of sorts. "Don't do all this on my account."

"You look exhausted." She pulled out a chair, watching him sip the strong coffee. She hovered.

Normally he hated such solicitousness, uncomfortable when anybody cared too much what he did or how he felt. In his book you judged a man by his actions, not his feelings. He'd done a lot in one day. He'd do more the next. As if it was all being added up on some ledger somewhere. Right now he was too tired to figure out how much he still owed.

An hour earlier he'd been up a pole, splicing wire and counting lightning strikes on the horizon, wondering how much time he had before one came down like God's finger and tapped him on the shoulder. He took chances a lot of the other guys wouldn't—as crew leader he wouldn't let them. But he survived. He always did. That was Zach Young—a survivor.

In the blurry lantern light he almost saw the newspaper clipping: "Joseph, 17, is survived by his parents, his sister Jean, and his brother Zachary."

"Zach?"

She'd said his name more than once and had refilled his cup. She smiled, as if his lapse in concentration was their secret. "Do you take sugar or cream?" The pink tip of her tongue darted out and wet her lips.

He didn't know if that was thunder thumping the ground or his heart kicking in.

"I swear I've put on three pounds this week thanks to real cream," she added. "Mrs. Griddell delivers it straight from her cows."

Zach knew there'd been a question back there somewhere, but by the time she gave him room to answer, he'd forgotten it. "Farming's hard work." He was clutching at straws.

She smiled wider. "So is being a lineman apparently."

"Yeah, well. Electricity has to be there when you flip the switch. People just don't know what to do without it."

"Back to the Dark Ages."

"Yeah. Huh." He laughed when the pun penetrated his brain but couldn't manage a smile. He dabbed a drop of rain from his cheek with the towel. Towel?

Sure, she'd draped it there on one of her whirlwind trips around the kitchen, slapped it around his shoulders, and said he looked drowned. The lingering impression of her hands remained on his shoulders, as if she'd been offering a massage he hadn't had the presence of mind to accept. For a surprising second regret coursed through him with the coffee. "You're taking mighty good care of me."

"It's the least—"

The lightning made her start. Not him. He deliberately set his coffee cup down and looked at his hands. The warmth of the lamplight, the light of her smile, stirred something in him, something that made him bone tired and wide-awake at the same time.

Coffee couldn't slake the familiar thirst. It started

in the back of his throat and tingled on his lips. He wanted a taste of her, for her to touch him again. But when her voice slowed to a halt, he knew it wasn't all sexual.

Keep talking, he prayed silently. He hadn't heard a woman's voice in a nighttime kitchen—it seemed like half his life. Someone telling him the details of her day. Someone to hold in bed when the talking was done. Something he'd never had and claimed he never would.

"You think it's safe?" she asked.

He thought nothing of the kind. "I gotta get going. You've been real kind."

She trailed him to the backdoor. "The line isn't sparking or anything, but I didn't know if that meant it was safe."

"What line?"

"The one that's down."

"You mean it's on the property?"

She pointed. In the blackness it didn't do much good.

He fetched the lantern from the table and held it high on the back porch. Firelight illuminated the rain like a thousand piercing needles. A black snake of line curled in an S at the base of the utility pole. Candace walked out into the yard, pointing at the barn roof and talking about a missing lightning rod.

Zach grabbed her around the waist and hauled her against him. "Stay back."

"But—"

"But nothing. A line doesn't have to spark to be live."

"Oh."

He gritted his teeth on a curse. She'd been all of five feet from stepping on it, and it had taken him that long to react. He ushered her back up the porch steps while rain tattled on the shingles.

"That's twice you've saved my life," she said, a trifle breathless.

"Twice?"

"Just being here is one. I hate being alone in the dark."

Funny, he thought, she had a voice that was made for the dark—low and even and precise. The woman had polish. She didn't belong on a farm any more than his arms belonged around her. He let her go and got his mind back on work.

He retrieved the voltage tester from his truck, pounded in a couple of warning stakes, and met her back on the porch. "Got any farm animals who might come across that line? Pets? What about a farmhand coming in in the morning?"

She shook her head and shrugged. "All by myself out here." She smiled, wiping her wet bangs off her forehead, never taking her eyes from his.

He thought he recognized the signals she was sending, but he was cautious enough to wait for more than one green light. She wasn't that old, maybe thirty; old enough to know an invitation when she made one.

"To be honest, Zach, I hate the idea of you driving home in this, there could be flash floods, trees down. I'd feel better if you spent the night here."

Green lights? That one lit up in neon.

He swayed toward her, barely lifting his hands where they hung heavy at his sides, touching the flare of her hips. Maybe it was the dark, the storm, maybe he couldn't figure it out just now, but he needed her, this peace in the middle of all hell breaking loose.

Her black eyes grew a fraction wider, and she stepped back across the threshold into the kitchen. "I meant on the couch, of course."

He rubbed the back of his neck, giving it a good

hard squeeze. Sleep deprivation playing with his mind. She'd made a neighborly offer, and he'd read way too much into it.

"You could sleep in my bed," she said. "I mean, I'd take the couch in that case. It's a long couch, but you're so tall—"

His wet clothes felt like a lead vest. His head was foggy and his hormones as reliable as a drunk driver walking a white line. He staggered inside. When a woman got going like that, you obeyed her every command. It was simpler that way.

Candy shooed him into the parlor with orders to sit down before he fell down. She stared after him, listening to him fumble in the dark, wondering if one week of seclusion had unhitched her brain cells. Had they gotten it straight about what her offer entailed? Judging by the weary glaze in his eyes, she wouldn't bet on it. But there was simply no way she'd send him back out in such weather.

"It was a dark and stormy night," she murmured, laughing at the melodrama. Two people stranded in a desolate farmhouse—some people would consider that a romantic situation. Unfortunately, she was one of them.

"Nonsense." The place was a mess, unpacked boxes stacked in every corner. Naturally she felt unsettled, uneasy; having a man handy made her feel a little safer. As for the wayward sparks going off between them at the strangest moments—"Too much electricity in the air," she decided, nodding once at the coffeepot on the old propane stove. Simply put, the lights were out and neither of them had anyplace else to be.

She hadn't asked if he was married, didn't need to. The man was as lonely as a coyote. He drank up her words as hungrily as her coffee. He looked at her the way a poor man stood on the wrong side of a jewelry-store window, knowing better than to even ask.

She recognized that look. The day after her divorce, glancing in a shop window on Fifth Avenue, she'd stared into the eyes of an unattached woman who looked an awful lot like her.

That was the day she'd hiked to Naomi's in the East Fifties and asked for the address of the defunct vegetable farm. Six months later she stood somewhere in the southeast corner of Kansas, cleaning up a year of barnyard neglect before she could even begin making the place pay off.

Poor Zach. He'd stumbled onto a woman simply desperate to find someone worse off than herself, helping people being the best cure she knew for getting her mind off her own troubles.

She entered the living room with the mugs of coffee. "Zach?" Her voice echoed off the high ceilings. The house felt cavernous and hollow.

Lightning flooded the room with jagged shadows as the front door slammed. A man's silhouette loomed in the doorway. Candy screamed.

"Who did you think it was?" Zach asked gruffly.

"You didn't answer."

"I hooked that banging shutter so we'd both get some sleep."

"Sorry. Thanks. Nerves, I guess." She set the tray beside the lantern on the coffee table. "I thought I'd make a fire. A little heat." A little light was more like it. "Fireplaces are so—" Romantic? She didn't finish the thought. "Have a seat."

Avoiding soaking the couch, he tugged on the knees of his work pants and perched on the edge of a cushion. White sheets and a pillow rested at the other end. "You got this set up fast."

Candy smiled stiffly. She wasn't *that* efficient. Living in a creaky farmhouse surrounded by nothing but fields and a windbreak of sighing trees, she'd spent every night on the sofa, a roaring fire making the flecked wallpaper dance, keeping scurrying shadows at bay. A few streetlights and a couple car alarms would've been more than welcome. So was Zach. This time she smiled happily and handed him a mug. "You sure you can sleep with all this coffee?"

He'd given up sleeping the minute he'd hauled her into his arms in the backyard. "You ought to have a lightning rod out there."

"The owners said it fell off."

"And batteries for your radio."

"I'll get right on it."

"It's a crime to let a farm get run-down like this."

"Sorry but I just got here myself."

And would go just as quickly, he thought glumly. City girls didn't take to the country for long. "Don't mind me. I get ornery when I'm tired. Just keep me off the Fate of the Family Farm."

Laughing, she crammed old newspapers into balls in the fireplace, tossing kindling on top of them. "I bet you want to get out of those clothes." She flashed him an apologetic smile, then spoke earnestly in the direction of the log pile. "You're soaked, and I have an old flannel robe, a big one. You'd be more comfortable. Drier. Warmer."

Zach ran a hand through his hair. If he got much warmer, his clothes would steam. *Was* she flirting, or had he been struck by lightning and he just didn't know it yet? It was nothing like the picture of limbo he'd heard about in Sunday school: a dark house, a night that wouldn't end, a beautiful woman flashing him looks he could've sworn . . .

She crouched in front of the fireplace, lit by the lantern on one side and flames on the other, womanly, rounded enough for a man to get his hands on something when he reached for her. Thanks to her apron he couldn't judge her front—

Hell and damnation, Young, why don't you ask her to get up and turn around a couple of times? He pictured her standing, seductively removing her blouse.

He stared furiously at the flames. She lit a good fire—it just had no business being in him.

"Hypnotizing, isn't it?" She stepped back and sat down. "I'll wait until it's caught, then I'll be off to bed."

He rubbed a hand over his mouth again, feeling the stubble of beard. "Sure thing."

"You'll be okay out here?"

"Fine."

"Good." Scooching forward to collect the coffee things, she patted his knee.

He set his hand firmly on hers and held it there. Maybe his imagination did all the inviting, but he had to be sure. His voice came out hoarse and none too certain. "What did you say your name was?"

"Candace." She valiantly ignored his grip. "Candace Wharton. Like the business school."

"Never heard of it."

Candy tried not to feel the heat of him, nor the muscle of his thigh tensing.

In her New York circle the little joke about her name went over well. It allowed whichever of her ex-husband's friends to launch into how or why he hadn't gotten into the nation's most prestigious business school and had chosen an Ivy League second best. It was an easy conversation opener—if you liked listening to men reciting their résumés.

Zach Young wasn't that kind of man. Sitting beside him as the storm raged, Candy wondered for a moment exactly what kind of man she'd allowed into her house.

Two

"Maybe I didn't make my offer clear, Zach."

He let her hand slip from under his. "You want me to go?"

She thought about it, crossing her arms loosely, aware for an instant of how her nipples contracted against the rain-spotted silk. Then lightning flashed again. She held herself tight until the thunder boomed, considering the faint flames and how dark the rest of the house was.

She finger-combed her hair, tipping her head to the side to air-dry it. "I'd like it if you stayed."

"Maybe that's the problem." The rasp of his voice made her want to clear her throat, clench her fists. He came imperceptibly nearer. "I'm too tired for games, Candy. If you're coming on to me, I'd like to know."

She didn't have an answer for that. She knew she'd been looking at him longer and harder than she normally would a stranger. *Because he looks so tired,* she answered her conscience.

And her smile? Just because it invited him to smile back didn't make it an invitation. Sharing a little human warmth could be a form of tenderness, of caring, of helping someone in need.

Despite the quivers of hesitation she wanted to reach out, to take the chance. She knew what it felt like to be on the outside looking in. Her isolation was voluntary. She sensed his wasn't. She could do something about that.

But it was the *way* she wanted to reach out that made her pause. Something about the currents coursing between them, sudden shocks of awareness. Her skin prickled and her blood hummed, tingling in her wrists until her hands itched to touch something. His face. His chest. She wanted to take his shoulders in her hands and press them back, to work that weary curve out of them, to stroke him. . . .

She shook her head. It had been a long time since she'd felt such a combination of headiness and excitement. And guilt. She had let him think he'd misunderstood her, probably because she didn't entirely understand herself. But the thought refused to go away: The man needed loving.

Candy Wharton wasn't sure she was the woman to give it to him. "You're tired. You should lie down."

"Beside you?"

She flushed and hoped he didn't see it. "On the couch. You need a place to sleep."

"Is that all?"

It wasn't *all* at all. She didn't know how or when, but she couldn't look him in the eye and deny it. It was like inviting the storm inside, glowering thunderheads looming on the horizon, invading the room.

"All right," he said softly, accepting her silence as an explanation. "I'd like to change out of these clothes."

She walked unsteadily into the bedroom, the walls growing and shrinking in the lantern light, shadows thrown across the flowered wallpaper, the double bed, and its nubby white spread. Nothing was certain in this cutoff nighttime world, not her house, not her own startling, explicit emotions.

Somehow she and Zach clicked, like the light switch she touched out of habit. The darkness remained.

He stood in the doorway behind her, his shoulders wide in the frame. She wet her lips again as she handed him the oversize flannel robe. "I don't know if this will fit."

"I'll try it."

"The bathroom's over there."

He followed her nod.

Stripping off his clothes in a pitch-black unfamiliar room, Zach banged his elbow against the sink and bit back a curse. He heard her bedroom door close.

"You scared her off for good." A guest didn't ingratiate himself by calling the hostess a tease. Had it been his imagination? Probably. From his bones outward he knew he looked like hell and smelled worse. He was too far gone for charm. He hadn't even thought of trotting out the arsenal of clumsy small talk he clung to on his infrequent dates.

Women usually liked him anyway; he'd never figured out why. The ones he dated were intelligent and quick enough to figure out after a month or two that he wouldn't be proposing. Any man who'd successfully sidestepped marriage for thirty-four years wasn't in a hurry to alter his ways.

He banged his shin on the toilet as he kicked off his work boots. Why was he so all-fired up to get back to her? Likely as not she'd locked her bedroom door by now, wedging a chair under the knob.

He peeled off his T-shirt and slung the robe around his shoulders. The seams stretched, a thread snapped.

He hung it on the doorknob, gathered up his clothes, and walked out wearing nothing but his shorts.

Candy sat on the floor with her back against the sofa, her knees drawn up. A sheepish smile curled her lips. "I know. I'm still here. I'll be gone any minute."

He backed toward the kitchen to grab a chair. Hauling it in front of the fire, setting it firmly between them, he draped his pants and shirt over it, stowing his work boots underneath. "It's your house. Stay as long as you like."

"It's kind of dark in there." She waved toward the black maw of the bedroom. "Can't see your hand in front of your face."

"You could leave the door open." He wondered if that wasn't exactly what she was doing.

He glanced at the living room her few pieces of furniture didn't quite fill. Shadows in the corners prodded him closer to the sofa. The primeval urge to huddle near the fire was as human in its way as the urge to reach for a woman in the dark.

Zach sat on the sofa, drawing the sheet across his lap and hunching forward, his elbows on his knees. A draft whispered across his bare shoulders. Lightning flashed in the distance, receding thunder sounded.

"Ten," they said simultaneously.

She flashed him a teasing smile. "You count the seconds between lightning and thunder, too?"

"It's automatic when you're up a pole."

"You don't go up when it's lightning!"

He'd done it twice that night. "If you're halfway through a job, in an emergency, the work gets done."

Jagged spears of light stabbed the earth. Candy didn't question the slivers of fear corkscrewing through her. Without thinking she reached up and placed her hand on his wrist. "Did anyone ever tell you you were a hero?"

He grimaced. "It's a job."

"A dangerous one." Lightning highlighted her hand on his skin. He looked down. She let go, getting up to throw another log on the fire. His gaze followed her—everywhere.

"I'm sorry to keep you up like this," she chatted. "Maybe it's the storm, charged ions or something. You need your sleep."

"I'd rather talk."

That kind of request she'd never deny. "About?"

"You. Living here. Meet any neighbors yet?"

She settled back on the floor, her arm almost grazing the side of his leg. He flexed his toes. She cupped her elbow in her hand so she couldn't accidentally skim the curled hairs on his leg, imagining them catching at the silk of her blouse, tugging.

She stared straight head. "I met Mrs. Griddell down the road. They've practically adopted me at the hardware store in Thayer. Fortunately Jeff, my ex-husband, granted me all the power tools in our divorce, and I'm pretty handy." She paused. "Never married, Zach?"

He shook his head.

She had to turn her head and glance back up at him. He shook it again, his gaze resting on hers. "Never."

The fire popped, spitting an ember onto the floor. Quickly, Candy got on her hands and knees and brushed it into the grate.

Zach grunted and stretched out, closing his eyes to the unintentional view of the softly molded half-moons of her derriere rounded by denim. He pulled the sheet over his feet and across his waist, wedging the pillow between the back of his head and the sofa arm. The pillowcase smelled of her. An ache rolled through him like distant thunder. He'd never pictured living with a woman, couldn't see one fitting into his life. Maybe that's why it shocked him how natural it felt, lying there, talking.

Then lust got all mixed up in it.

They stayed quiet for a few minutes, tension winding through the air like a thin stream of smoke, obvious and insubstantial. The merest breeze would dissipate it. He inhaled her scent on the pillowcase, watching the outline of her face as she studied the fire. Apparently she didn't want to leave any more than he wanted her to go.

He almost said her name. He stared at the ceiling instead, and the words began, surprising them both. He talked about outages and crews. How they covered four counties with twenty linemen. How long they'd been working and how hard and how the adrenaline of a storm pumped you up but didn't last forever. Stuff he never talked about because his coworkers knew it already and anyone else might think he was complaining.

"We've got the hospital at Parsons and an old-folks home with life-support systems, people with baby monitors and refrigerated insulin. Without power it all stops. Traffic lights, electronic jail cells, even the sliding doors at the grocery . . ." He wanted to persuade her it wasn't such a big deal, no heroics. "If we do it right, you never even notice us."

Candy touched her fingertips to her lips. The man had spent the evening risking his life so she could sit there obliviously enjoying a slice of strawberry cheesecake and carping about bad radio reception. And he said he wasn't a hero!

Maybe that's why the emotional draw was as elemental as the physical one, she thought suddenly. Maybe that's why it was so imperative that she help him. He was too good a man to be so alone.

Outside another storm front gathered its forces. The wind howled, hail pattering the house.

Candy heard Zach yawn, felt him stretch. She'd kept her eyes steady on the fire when he'd walked out of the bathroom. That didn't stop her remembering. Firelight had defined his chest muscles, sleek and smooth. Whorls of sandy hair circled dark caramel nipples, glinting against tanned skin. In the dimness her eye had been drawn immediately to the white of his shorts, the power of his legs.

She should say good night. She didn't.

She'd known him barely an hour and trusted him with her life. Why? Because he'd risked his and hadn't even asked for a thank you. Because when she told him she didn't want him, he'd respected that.

She warmed her palms by rubbing them together. She wanted to smooth his face, ease the tired lines, kiss just a corner of his mouth, and see him smile. To feel the intensity that had sparked between them when he'd held her hand to his leg and said, What do you want, Candy?

She wanted him.

Candy Wharton did not believe in one-night stands. But she believed in helping people. If someone needed food, you fed him. Shelter, clothing, a listening ear, if it was hers to give, she gave.

The wailing storm, the enveloping dark, was no excuse for the fantasies flashing through her mind. She talked instead, hoping he'd drift off to sleep and not make her face the scandalous turn her senses had taken. "I moved from New York last week. That was a laugh and a half. First there was the van crisis, the tollbooth crisis, the brake-light thing . . ."

She made listening easy, Zach thought, her voice clear and crisp. His grammar was lazy in comparison. Of course he could fix it up anytime, speak a little more properly. His jaw clenched. He'd barely met her, and he was changing his life to impress her. He punched the pillow.

"Comfortable?" she asked, turning her head.

"Sure." He was wide-awake and dreaming, that's all. Dreaming about a woman who cared whether his pillow was fluffed enough, who acted as if what he wanted mattered. As if *he* mattered.

Taking care of other people was his job—it was as natural to him as breathing. Being on the receiving end was new, eye-opening, seductive. He pictured them side by side in bed, her voice soothing him to sleep.

But a man didn't always want soothing. Late night harbored its own lullabies. Almost without meaning to, he touched her hair where it spread on the cushion at the base of her neck, skimming it between his finger and thumb. When he not so accidentally grazed her neck, her stream of quiet talk stopped.

The new line of storms loomed overhead. Nature howled and the frame house whistled and groaned. A shutter smacked the boards outside, the known world coming apart piece by piece. Zach's breathing got slow and even. Candy turned and looked at him.

She swallowed and tried to remember where in her silly story she'd left off. "Did I tell you about the tollbooth?"

He shook his head back and forth, his hair whispering on the pillow. "Tell me."

Her voice got hoarse and catchy. "Uh, in Illinois, I . . ." She couldn't think, not with his fingers skittering back and forth under her hair. She touched his hand, lightly leading it to her shoulder.

"Sorry." He lifted it away.

She caught it back.

"Candy." His voice held a warning she didn't heed.

"I want to say thank you."

"You don't owe me."

No? She had to offer. "I know what I want, Zach." She said his name on purpose, her gaze meeting his. His eyes were a warm brown, framed by sandy lashes. "I just don't know how to say it without sounding—"

Her voice broke off as she concentrated on the large male hand she held between both of hers. She turned it over, brushing the backs of his knuckles with the tip of her nose, then her lips. She placed a soft reverent kiss in his palm.

To Zach it felt like catching a butterfly. Then the back of her fingers traced the scratchy beginnings of a beard.

"What do you want?" he asked, his voice raspy.

"To give you what you need."

"That would be . . . ?"

"Caring." She feathered her fingers down his throat. He knew she felt him swallow. "Is that what you call this?"

She raised her shoulder in a light shrug. "Tenderness then?"

"Touching?" He drew her hand to his chest, the boom of a heartbeat. His hand clasped around hers and threatened to move it lower.

She withdrew, something like embarrassment flickering over her features. "I didn't mean it that way."

"Didn't you?" He came up on one elbow, frowning when she shrank back. He knew damn well what she meant—she was offering him more than just sex. Not love, not so soon, but something. Besides, love was for other people, not him. Either way it was a gift he didn't deserve.

His dry husky laugh rumbled in the room. "You want to give me something? Heat me up a glass of warm milk."

"I think you need more than that."

"And you're it?"

She wouldn't look away this time. Her eyes were like black buttons, her face oval and pale in the dim light. Two circles of pink stood out on her cheeks—from the flames within or without, he couldn't tell. "Are you always this cautious, Zach?"

He tried to be. That bad things happened when you least expected them was a given in his life. That good things could happen the same way was harder to accept. "I'm not saying no."

She laughed. "You're not saying yes either."

He waited too long. She got skittish.

Twisting a strand of hair around her finger, looking in all the dark corners, she said, "I'm sorry. I've made a fool of myself and made you very uncomfortable."

"Do I look uncomfortable?" He smiled on purpose, stretching out a kink in his lower back by lifting his hips. He cocked one arm above his head, his chest rising and falling as he kept his breathing even and made room on the sofa. "Go ahead," he said. "I won't bite."

She didn't move.

"Unless you want me to." He winked.

He didn't want her feeling bad. Not when she'd had the guts to make the offer in the first place. Especially not when the idea finally penetrated his foggy brain that maybe *she* was the one who needed *him*. A woman in need, now that he understood. He'd just never met one quite like her before.

She perched on the edge of the cushion without letting her rear end come in contact with his thighs.

"Did your ex call you Candy?"

She shook her head, a flash of lightning burnishing her hair with blue highlights. "Candace."

"Which do you like?"

"Candy." Her voice was barely a whisper. "Thank you for asking."

Zach rubbed her back for a minute, then said something he didn't even know he'd been thinking. "He didn't hurt you, did he?"

"My ex? Oh no. I divorced *him*."

The whys echoed through his mind settling down to one. "Why me?"

He expected something about her being on the rebound, about self-esteem or boldly shedding old ways. She smiled and let her fingers skim the lazy curls of his chest hair. "Would you believe me if I said you were a good man and you deserve all the loving you haven't been getting?"

"Do I look that desperate?"

"You've been a perfect gentleman so far."

"Then I must be doin' somethin' wrong." He sat up so close, his chest almost brushed hers. "Don't run away now."

"I won't."

Unsure, a little scared, those black eyes had fooled him for a minute. He thought she was going to change her mind. He tilted his head, watching her do the same in the opposite direction. Their lips came together lightly. Hand on her back, he pressed her softly to him.

When he released her, he looked into eyes as black as the sky outside. Maybe they'd always be that color. Maybe in the light of day they'd carry the night with them. He wanted it to be this night. Any woman brave enough to lay it on the line the way she had deserved the best he could give.

He kissed her again. His heart slammed against his ribs as she leaned in cautiously and kissed him back. He held his breath, as if waiting for lightning to strike again. When her tongue touched his, it did.

They opened their mouths. Exploration took time;

they paused, asked silent questions, gave each other permission to go further. He threaded his fingers through the silky night of her hair. Her head fell back, and she smiled faintly. When he ran his hand up and down her arm a couple of times, she moved it to her breast.

He couldn't have said her name if he'd wanted to. It was as if they'd fallen off the edge of the earth, the only two people in the whole world. Why wasn't important anymore. Walking into her kitchen, he hadn't questioned why he'd felt instantly at home. He just had. The sensations burning through him were every bit as real, as undeniable.

She unbuttoned her blouse, parting the silk folds. "I don't usually do things like this. I want you to know that."

"Neither do I." Except in his dreams.

He ran his hand over body-warm lace, cupping her, kissing the smooth slope of her chest, the cool gold of a fine chain around her neck, taking the pert tip of a breast in his mouth at last.

He awoke with a groan. That had been the hottest, most exhausting dream. . . . He sat up fast. "Hey, what time is it?"

He heard her clattering in the kitchen. Light streamed into the nearly bare white living room. The scent of bacon and eggs wafted by. He heard the sizzle of butter in a pan. He was in her house all right. That part had been real.

She breezed through, looking chipper and carelessly elegant in slacks and a polo shirt. "It's nine A.M. Rise and—"

"Nine! Holy—" He started to get up, remembered the condition he was in, and grabbed the sheet around him. No sense imposing a morning erection on the lady just because she'd starred in some of the wildest erotic dreams he'd had since puberty. "Where're my clothes?"

"Don't worry. I heard the radio in your truck crackling, so I answered it. They said Wichita had sent over two crews, and you could sleep until ten if you felt like it."

She'd talked to the office. That voice, that diction. Everyone would ask him who the woman was and how he'd come to spend the night— He held his head in his hands and took a deep rib-expanding breath. It'd be fine as long as he stuck to the facts. The sooner he forgot that slow-mo replay of erotic fantasy that had haunted him all night, the better he'd be.

She plopped a neatly folded pile of clothes on the end of the sofa. "Ironed, not starched. I have a battery travel iron."

"You didn't have to—"

"Not another word. They needed it."

He needed his head examined.

She waltzed away.

He squinted at the blazing sunshine outside and did her the favor of not salivating over her retreating figure. Who needed a woman in slacks when he had a picture in his head of her naked, hefted in his hands, caressed. . . .

He grabbed his clothes and sprinted into the bathroom.

"The water heater's off," she called out, making it sound like birdsong. "Beware of cold showers!"

He would've loved one if he'd had the time.

Wincing at the bright light bouncing off the white tile walls, he braced his hands on either side of the porcelain sink. The woman hadn't scurried at first sight of him, hadn't draped herself all over him, hadn't waited for some mention of the previous night or a morning-after summation. She'd acted perfectly normal and natural.

A dream, it had to be.

He reached for the faucet, his hand freezing in midair. Wound around two of his fingers was a thin gold chain. Hers.

It had happened the second time. He'd gotten a little carried away, a little rough, grasping her neck so hard, the tiny filigree had snapped. She hadn't cared, not at the time. At the time the roof could have blown off and neither would have done anything but strain toward the stars—they'd been halfway there anyway.

"The second time," he said with a moan, fixing a glare at the man in the mirror.

The memory of the first time came back clear as ice.

He'd touched her breast, licked it, had taken most of her in his mouth, and done his damnedest to pay homage to the rest. She was pink and pebbled. Standing in front of the mirror, he could almost taste her.

Then he'd leaned back, pulling her down on his chest. She'd come willingly, shedding her blouse in the firelight so she could skim her sensitive nipples against him.

Under her blouse, under her discarded jeans, she wore a one-piece lavender teddy, not too many ribbons or frills, just a hot smooth satin across her stomach. Lace cups shaped the bra, lace rode high on her legs. She'd stood up to show him, turning slowly in a circle, one minute illuminated in red firelight, the next in white lightning.

He'd asked for his wallet. She'd gotten it, opening it to the bulge where he kept a condom. She'd torn it open. With her teeth.

Zach's back stiffened just thinking of it. He rested

his forehead against the mirror. Ruthlessly he twisted the cold-water faucet and shoved the plug in. Sparkling cold water didn't blunt the memory of flames and shadows and a dark angel hovering over him.

In the light of day words and images came back, garbled with praise and murmured pleas.

"You won't think I'm the wrong kind of woman," she'd asked.

"You couldn't be righter."

She'd laughed. He'd known he was going to love that laugh before he'd ever heard it.

Breath choked in his throat when she'd knelt beside him, directing his hand between her legs to show him how to unsnap the snaps on the teddy. He'd peeled it up over her hips, loving her there, laving her, stroking her. She'd arched in his hands.

When her shuddering had subsided, she'd lifted one knee across his waist, straddling him. "Okay?"

As if she'd had to ask.

The first time they'd been gentle, giving freely but testing, too, a little unsure how far to go, how much to reveal. The second time had been lightning and thunder and nature's fury unleashed. He'd broken that golden chain. She'd—

He only carried one condom in his wallet. What had they used the second time? He racked his foggy brain. Suddenly he remembered, pressing his forehead to the glass with a groan.

"You okay in there?"

Her sunny morning voice shocked him, and he snapped off the water before it could lap over the edges of the sink.

"Fine," he growled.

"Breakfast will be done in a second."

"I don't know if I'll have time."

He waited for her reaction. Petulance? Tense silence?

Whistling. She whistled as she trod lightly into the other room.

He looped the gold chain over the antique light fixture beside the mirror. There was only one thing to do about it now. He took a deep breath and plunged his face ear-deep into the icy water.

Three

He'd steeled himself to the idea of a big breakfast, one of the tense expectant kinds with her sitting across the table watching every bite. Candy congratulated herself on not giving it to him. Driving down the road to Grace Griddell's farm, she mentally patted herself on the back for simply handing the man a brown bag of biscuits, a container of scrambled eggs with bacon crumbled on top, and a thermos she'd retrieved from his truck, brimming with coffee. "There you go," she'd said.

And there he'd went.

Candy breathed a sigh of relief and slowed for a bump in the road, feeling out her emotions.

"Candace Wharton, what you did was darn near unforgivable, not to mention dangerous, careless, and . . . promiscuous!" Promiscuity and Candy were such an unlikely pair, it took her a minute even to come up with the word.

Try as she might, she couldn't understand why the night before had felt, still felt, so inevitably right. He'd been so easy to love, to give to.

"And you gave him just about everything. Shameless hussy." She gripped the steering wheel, suppressing a guffaw. The insult just didn't fit.

She didn't feel ashamed, she felt—fine. Sunny. Physically every corner of her body felt the impress of his, the graze of flesh against flesh, the breached secrecy of private places. Inside she felt buoyant, like a rainbow on the horizon. It had to be the ions in the air. She pictured them dancing like motes in the morning sun.

Her only regret seemed to be that she didn't feel *more* regret. "Women who sleep with strange men really shouldn't feel so good about it," she reminded herself sternly.

Up since six that morning, pressing clothes she didn't have time to wash, whipping up a breakfast she couldn't eat, she'd run through every possible definition of how she *should* feel. She'd quickly dismissed the silly notion of love at first sight. Lust was more like it. Two adults on a stormy night, things had gotten out of hand. Twice.

But lust wasn't it. Was she on the rebound? That didn't ring true either. Despite every aching, satisfied inch of her body lust and storms had been but a part of it.

She recalled Zach's creased face, the weariness he'd carried into her kitchen. Theirs had been an emotional coming together. It wasn't his hand on her breast, it was what that hand meant, his reaching out, their sharing, the surprising fulfillment she'd found meeting that need.

Turning into Grace's drive, Candy switched off the radio, realizing she hadn't heard a lick of music.

The spanking neatness of the Griddell farm reminded her she'd come to Kansas to begin her second life, a solitary satisfying one. Looking across the farmland, the word *barren* grated on her. Just because she couldn't have children, couldn't hope to have a normal marriage and family life, didn't mean she'd be unproductive. She could make things grow, nourishing, healthy things. She could contribute.

"You gonna sit there listening to the grass grow?" With a shovel in her hands Grace Griddell stood in the doorway of her barn, the pockets of her denim overalls stuffed with gloves, tools, and tissues.

"'Morning!" Candy jumped down from her little truck and patted Shepherd, the arthritic farm dog, gingerly stepping over a half-dozen barn cats lolling in the sun. "Did you have any damage last night?"

"None to speak of. Looks like you were up."

And over and under. Candy felt her cheeks turn red and played with the bandanna holding her hair off her face, fingering the knot at the back of her neck. "It was stormy all right."

"Had a tornado touch down north of town."

"No!"

"No one hurt, but a few families from the trailer park are camped out in the high-school gym. I'm baking bread right now."

"What can I do to help?" Candy asked instantly.

"Pick up some wood and come on in."

After they fed the wood-burning cookstove in Grace's kitchen, Candy got to work kneading three bowls of rising dough. Useful activity was as welcome as Grace's friendship. She admired the older woman immensely. But a person could hardly come right out and say, "I want to be you when I grow up."

Grace was approximately fifty, savvy, competent, self-sufficient. She'd run the farm single-handedly since her husband's death ten years ago. She wore whatever it took, overalls and rubber boots for cleaning out the barn, a flowered dress for choir practice in town. Her one concession to femininity was her iron-gray hair, fluffed and hairsprayed to withstand anything. She had no children. She was happy.

"You pitch right in," Grace said.

"Best way to make friends is to be one," Candy replied. "My father's a pastor; sometimes I think in sermons."

"Strict?"

"Loving," she answered without hesitation. "He always said, 'Love the people who need it most.'" Would he have approved of Zach? she wondered. Candy stopped kneading for a moment.

"How'd you make out last night?" Grace asked.

Candy blinked, aghast at the deep welts her fingers made in the dough. She hurriedly stretched the loaf into an unrecognizable blob and started over. "Pardon me?"

"With the farm."

"I have a line down. Did you lose power?"

"Would I be using the woodstove if I hadn't? Which one was he?"

Candy's throat went dry. News traveled fast in small towns, but this was ridiculous.

"Saw a Prairieland truck go by this morning," Grace said, wiping flour from a corner of the long pine table with a damp rag. "Thought he came from your place."

"A lineman." Candy grabbed a big knife to cut a mound of dough into two loaves. "He came by last night." She couldn't lie to this woman. She had the sinking feeling it wouldn't help if she did—Grace was shrewd. "He slept over—due to the storm. Zach Young. Do you know him?"

"Guess you do, too. Now."

Candy smiled; the twinkle in Grace's eye seemed to call for it. Thankfully the woman didn't prod anymore, and they worked in companionable silence. Companionable for Grace perhaps, unfocused and dreamy for Candy.

"So what'd he do?"

What didn't he do? Candy thought. "He staked the downed line. Had some coffee. Slept on the sofa. Did you know the bridge was out?"

"There's gotta be more than that."

"We talked a bit."

"I meant the county road is washed out in three places and there's a bridge at Star River that's gonna take a crane to resurrect. I think that one's done, honey."

Stricken, Candy spotted eight plump loaves set out on Grace's end of the table. For her part she'd successfully mangled one piece of tired dough into submission. "Sorry."

"You do what you can."

Candy looked into the older woman's eyes a moment, wondering if she'd meant that to sound as wise and far-reaching as it had.

Grace used the old pump handle in the sink to get some water flowing and rinsed her hands, carefully tucking a strand of hair into place. "That was mighty friendly of him. Staying the night."

Friendly was hardly the word for it, Candy thought. She'd never opened herself to a man the way she had to him. She firmly believed real love took time, a buildup of experiences and beliefs. But what happened when disappointments and resentments built up too? She'd been such a disappointment to Jeff. He'd tried to accept her sterility. She'd thought divorcing him was the kindest, noblest thing she could do. Obviously he'd found other ways of coping long before that.

She dumped a loaf into a pan to rise, covering it with a dishtowel like a sheet over a corpse. Jeff, Zach, all of it was history.

While Grace went to the cellar to retrieve some jam to send into town with the loaves of bread coming out of the oven, Candy sipped her second coffee of the day, determined not to let the flavor remind her of Zach's kisses.

"Our mistakes don't have to haunt us if we learn from them," her father would say. What she'd learned was that sex, without the emotional baggage of a relationship gone awry, was freer and more exciting than anything she'd ever experienced.

Because there were no strings attached, she insisted silently. *Because* it began and ended there. Zach had known that when he'd scooted out that morning; she knew it. It was over.

"You going to put that in a pan or burp it?"

Candy realized she'd been bouncing a rounded loaf in her hands while lost in thought. "Sorry." She laughed. "Didn't get much sleep last night."

"That downed power line could've started a fire."

Candy couldn't say it hadn't.

As she helped Grace fix lunch they finally got around to talking about Candy's farm. She'd plant in three weeks, the weather being as wet as it was, staggering the crops so her output to New York would be continuous. Grace gave her the names of seed suppliers and recommended a family called Lamont for organic fertilizer.

After lunch, her truck cab loaded with warm loaves of bread, Candy headed to the high school then on to the hardware and grocery stores. Along the way she reached a conclusion about Zach Young. He'd needed her help as much as those people at the school had, and she'd offered it. But there'd be no relationship, certainly no sexual dalliance. If she had to, she'd tell him so. From the way he'd taken off that morning she figured he'd already gotten the message. The man was as shy of involvement as she was dead set against it.

A clean break. No loose ends. Her new life would get a new beginning.

• • •

When she turned into her driveway at the end of the afternoon, she slammed on the brakes so hard, her bag of groceries pitched forward. Two squat yellow line trucks sat in her yard.

Her heart thumped. Her breath wheezed out of her lungs like the hydraulics on the cherry picker as its basket lifted a man to the top of the pole. They were repairing her line.

"Talk about tying up loose ends," Candy muttered, easing her suddenly sweaty palms off the steering wheel. She hopped down from her truck, the tiny import model looking like a toy beside the utility vehicles.

"Howdy," she said, the bag of groceries crushed in her arm.

A new slant on the previous night occurred to her with sickening clarity. What if he bragged about it? Her blood ran cold. *Oh Candy, you knew there'd be consequences.*

However, the five men merely nodded her way, their hard hats dipping in unison.

"Fixing your line," one of them said.

"So I see."

"Should have it done in an hour at the most."

"Thank you."

She headed into the house, breathless and queasy. Throwing out a handful of defrosted frozen dinners, she tossed her purchases in the lukewarm refrigerator and slammed the door. "You can't hide in here," she insisted, wanting nothing more than to stick her head in the dripping freezer and keep it there.

"Besides, if he's that kind of man, I'll eat my socks." Whatever out-of-this-world attraction had overtaken them, trust had been part of it.

"You trusted Jeff too." She bit her lip and resolutely turned a scowl into a smile. Pulling back her shoulders, she walked out onto the back porch, watching the work in progress. Rather than mosey over to the working men, she turned a sharp right and paced around the house, inspecting for damage.

A couple of shutters hung atilt on the second story. A patch of shingles had flown off. She'd probably find them in the next field over. Once more she toted up the cost of paint for the peeling south side of the house. In bright sunlight the place was more dilapidated than she liked to admit.

"'Afternoon," Zach said.

All at once her heart felt as big and empty as the blue sky, waiting for breath, air, something to fill it. She turned. "Hello."

"Hello again." He smiled.

He looked wonderful. Taller than she'd remembered. His shoulders had lost their stoop, his neck unbowed by exhaustion. His narrow hips were canted slightly by the way he stood, one knee bent, the toe of his boot pointing up as he dug his heel into the damp ground beside the overgrown rosebush.

"I was in the truck figuring out your work order when you drove up." He slapped an aluminum clipboard against his thigh several times. A pen, tied to it with twine, tapped his leg. He stuck it in the clip.

"I thought I wasn't high on the list of priorities," Candy said.

"Well, there's priorities and there's priorities."

Candy planted her feet firmly. "Mr. Young, there are ten families living in the high-school gym. I'd give them a place to stay myself, if the upstairs didn't leak. I can't accept favoritism simply because we—" She stammered to a halt, staring at him fiercely, as if it was his fault she couldn't finish the sentence.

He tipped his hard hat back. "You being a city girl, I figured you'd be out of here inside twenty-four hours if we didn't have your MTV hooked back up." He grinned, more at the rosebush than at her, and took his hat off, wiping his forehead with his sleeve.

His hair was a lighter shade of auburn than she remembered. Lank with sweat, it had been wet and combed slick that morning. She remembered the droplet that had run down his cheek as he'd accepted her breakfast to go. She'd been tempted to wipe it away.

She wouldn't be tempted again. "I don't have cable, and it'll take more than a power outage to chase me off."

He squinted over a field of spring cornstalks, looking the slightest bit disappointed. Candy wished his eyes weren't precisely the color of Grace's roan mare, they'd be too easy to remember during the nights to come. His smooth cheek showed he'd found time to shave. Stubble vanished more easily than the pale red abrasion on her breasts, which tingled even now.

"Actually the favoritism is on my account," Zach said. "My folks live at the end of this line. Ma runs a day-care. When we considered the families leaving their kids off, and Grace Griddell cooking up a storm for the Hastings Park people, we bumped this up."

Chastened, Candy rubbed her arms, inhaling a rush of damp air. "I didn't mean to tell you your business."

"A downed line is a safety hazard."

"You said it was dead."

"For now. If someone turns on a home generator without throwing the breakers, all that juice can feed back down the line, and suddenly you've got a problem."

Candy knew nothing about generators. "Grace has one. For her milking machine."

"A lot of people know what precautions to take. It's

just when the lights go out, people don't always think the way they do in the daytime." He looked at her now, the wind dying to a whisper, the air buzzing with the distant sound of machinery. They were on the far side of the house. It could have been the far side of the moon. "Things become more urgent in the dark."

It was Candy's turn to look away. She stared at the house, peeling paint off it in strips.

Zach came up beside her, a head taller, his body warm. He flicked a finger over the bare board, tapping. "Looks firm, reliable."

So did he, Candy thought.

A man in a hurry strode around the corner of the house, a question half asked by the time he reached Zach. Zach was in mid-answer when the man nodded, muttered, "I told 'em so," and turned on his heel.

Candy laughed. "Such efficiency."

"They know their stuff."

"Guess I got lucky last night, having you stop by."

A smile flickered around the edges of his eyes, the lines creasing faintly. "I think we both got lucky."

"Zach."

"Candy."

For a second they listened to the sound of their names on each other's lips.

"Candy, I'm not about to broadcast it. I just wanted you to know I appreciated last night." Appreciated! He snapped a thorn off a rosebush branch. "I mean, I appreciate that you're not the kind of woman who—"

"Never."

"Me either. I don't usually take advantage, I mean, I won't, in case you were worried—"

"Me? No, I wasn't—I mean, it's fine if you—" Good Lord, she was picking up his speech patterns. She took a deep breath. "I realize it won't happen again, Zach. I wasn't expecting it to."

His chin came up a fraction when he pricked his thumb on another thorn. "Good. We got that straight."

Candy breathed easier. She'd been right to trust him. Liking him seemed to follow as naturally as breathing. "It's very thoughtful of you to reassure me."

Reassurance had nothing to do with it, Zach thought. Oh, he could shoot the bull with the best of them, convince himself it was the gentlemanly thing to do, maybe cover his tracks by being sure she wasn't going to report him to the general manager or something. But underneath it all he'd simply wanted to see her again. Make sure she hadn't been a dream.

It wasn't until he'd come around the corner of the house and seen her standing there, hair fluttering in the breeze, her trim cable-knit sweater covering a body he remembered in every detail, that he'd known how wrong he'd been to come. And how useless it would have been to resist.

He had to see her. Fix that line for her. Check out the connections. Make sure she was okay.

"Gotta check on the crew." He sidled back to the sunny side of the house.

"Sure." She strolled along beside him until they were even with the first truck.

"Just wanted to welcome you to the area," he said, formally shaking her hand.

"That's some welcome wagon," she muttered.

He coughed into his fist rather than laugh.

Candy tucked a windswept hair into her red bandanna, a devilish twinkle in her eye. "I'm glad this is all fixed, Zach. Thanks."

She watched them splice the new line and found herself listening to Zach as he directed his crew, his voice rustling up and down her skin.

He wore denim and a flannel shirt, sleeves rolled up his forearms. As he walked over to the other crew leader, she noted the gloves stuck in his back pocket. She saw the bulge of his wallet at his hip and wondered if he'd gotten another condom. She flushed. But when he came back to stand beside her, she couldn't stop herself from saying one more thing. "Zach?"

"Yeah?"

She put her hand on his arm, raising the other to shade her eyes. "I'm glad I could help. You look good, much better."

Zach knew she wouldn't flatter him. His heart clutched in his chest anyway. He wanted to preen and strut and tell the whole crew this shiny elegant woman from New York had called him, what? Better?

He had a ton of work to do. He could be out of there in five minutes if he left the cleanup to Brian Macklin's crew. Instead he stood around, unable to resist the urge to tease her. "I looked that bad, huh?"

"You looked tired."

"It's a wonder you let me in." He didn't wink. She got the double entendre before he did.

"You look healthier," she said firmly.

"You're telling me I was sickly?"

Candy laughed. "You know darn well what I mean, and I won't help you fish for any more compliments." She tossed her head and threw him a smile over her shoulder as she stalked toward the house. "Think your men would like some lemonade?" she called. "I got a bag of ice in town."

"Thanks, but we'll be out of your hair in a minute."

"You all be careful now." She scampered up the stairs into her suddenly sunny kitchen and took a deep cleansing breath.

Hands on hips she scanned the room, realizing at

last how easily she could make this place a home with a little elbow grease, some wallpaper, and paint. For some reason she had the energy to do it all right then. Filling a bucket with oil soap and grabbing a sponge, she got started on the living room, glancing up to watch the trucks pull out.

If her euphoria had anything to do with Zach Young's rested appearance, or his smile, or his quiet concern for her, she figured that was simply pride in a job well done. As her father would say, "Helping others has its rewards."

She waved a big orange sponge at them as they drove away.

Normally Zach wouldn't have thought twice about a customer waving them off, most people were thrilled to have the lights back on. What bothered him was the way he'd stared in his side-view mirror all the way down the drive, hoping to catch sight of her.

"She's a looker," Tom Warsaw said, running a hand through his gunmetal-gray brush cut—a left-over, Zach swore, from the Korean War.

Tom was the eldest member of Zach's three-man crew, prematurely gray, and putting on weight. Beside him sat Jerry Sczcypka, who was as wiry as a stray dog. The newly graduated apprentice had been welcomed as part of a pair instantly dubbed Tom and Jerry.

Both men eyed Zach inquiringly. He concentrated on the road.

"Not b-bad," Jerry suggested, his slight stutter worsening whenever it came to women. "If you like b-brunettes."

"You stayed at her place last night," Tom stated.

"Had to stay somewhere." Zach tried to keep the

annoyance out of his voice when the silence stretched. "Hey, did I say anything happened?"

"We didn't say anything," they replied in tandem.

"N-no."

"Hell, no."

They watched the corn go by.

"She make you breakfast?" Tom asked.

Zach scowled at the sun glinting off the pavement. Hell yes, she'd made him breakfast. Why did answering that question seem like a full-blown confession? "Damn!" He slapped the steering wheel. "Hand me that brown bag, would you?"

Jerry fished it out from under the front seat. Without a word Zach tucked it in the pocket of the door and reminded himself to take back her container. He could have done it earlier, gotten it out of the way. She probably wanted it back soon.

He mentally scanned his schedule. They had another four hours of work at least. It'd be late by the time he stopped at his place and showered. He'd check on Ma and Pa on the way. Not that he worried; they knew more than he ever would about weathering storms.

When it was too late to stick around, too late to invite himself in, too late to do anything but say "Here's your bowl," he'd stop by her place, hand her the paper bag, and run.

Should he wash it out first?

He glanced automatically at the metal numbers nailed to the poles alongside the road, counting down as they neared the county line. He'd known her all of eighteen hours, and he was worrying about washing her dishes. What a woman couldn't do to a man!

Four

Zach stood on her back porch feeling like a scare-crow in a new suit. The pulse in his neck pounded against a too-tight collar. Flowers. He should have a bouquet of flowers in his hand instead of this silly plastic box with the burpable lid. It wasn't much to hand a lady.

The way she beamed up at him through the back-door window, it could've been a dozen roses. "Zach!"

He half turned as she opened the door, ready to flee at a moment's notice. He sidled close enough to hand the thing to her. "Just wanted to bring this back. Thanks again." He didn't say for what.

"You're not running away, are you?"

How in blazes could a man answer that question?

"Come on in." She looked him up and down. "Unless you have a date."

He grabbed the unbuttoned sides of his sport coat. "Kind of chilly out here," he said.

"Then by all means come inside."

Shuffling into her shiny clean kitchen, he watched his boot tracks outlining his retreat route.

"Did you work late?" she asked.

"Until seven."

She smiled. Her cheeks shone like the kitchen, scrubbed and clean and pink. If she wore makeup it was the see-through kind. Her eyes were black but somehow soothing, like a deep starry sky. He got the idea he could look into them and see all the way to her soul, and she'd let him.

He did a quick reconnaissance of the kitchen. "Smells great in here."

"Oil soap and freshly baked pies. I've embraced domesticity with a vengeance."

He saw the pies on the counter, about a dozen. "For the people in town?"

"Exactly. Grace gave me the canned cherries, and I did the rest. Seemed the least I could do since I got my power turned on so much earlier than I'd expected." She batted her lashes.

"I don't want you to think we did anything out of line. Like I said—"

"You were very gracious to explain it so patiently, Zach. I was a boor to accuse you of favoritism when there you were, well, doing me a such favor. I've been wanting to apologize all day."

Zach cleared his throat, wishing she wouldn't look up at him and let her voice get all soft and silky. "You've got nothing to apologize for."

She'd been thinking about him. He'd been thinking about her, unable to shake this feeling that dogged him all day, wanting to be there in her kitchen with her. He stepped toward the living room. "Looks different in the daylight, doesn't it?"

"The Jetsons meet Ma and Pa Kettle," a merry voice said behind him. "Half the knickknacks are the former owners', the fifties decor is all mine. My ex decided to completely redecorate once his new wife— well, I liked these pieces, so I brought them with me."

She was settling in. Maybe she'd stick around, Zach thought. "Life returns to normal pretty fast once the lights go back on."

"That's very true. That doesn't mean people should forget what it's like without them."

He supposed she meant the row of candles on the mantel, the fire-engine-red lantern next to the door. All the same he couldn't stop thinking she meant him and what had happened in that room.

They caught each other staring at the silvery ashes in the fireplace.

"Haven't had the radio off yet," Candy said, striding briskly into the kitchen to turn it down. "Make Me Your Baby" wasn't a song she wanted to hear right now.

"No, leave it on." He followed her, his shoulders filling the doorway. "My grandmother says when they first got electricity in the late thirties, she had to chase the farmhands out of the yard with a broomstick or they'd spend all day listening to old radio shows." He frowned. "Though I suppose they were new then."

She chuckled. "They didn't get electricity until the 1930s?"

"Not outside of town. There're plenty of people around here who remember heating water on the stove for a Saturday-night bath, reading by kerosene lamps, getting a fire going for the evening. Every night would've been like last night."

Her eyes widened a bit, and she turned down the corners of her mouth to hide a smile. "Now that would be hard to imagine."

They both burst out laughing. His deep chuckle bounced off the cabinets.

"No wonder those women were old before their time," Candy exclaimed, a slight flush coloring her cheeks.

Zach leaned an elbow on the counter and eyed the pies. In his haste to do everything he possibly could to delay getting there, he'd forgotten to eat. It was almost eight-thirty and they'd run out of small talk already. His stomach obliged, filling the silence with a growl.

"Say no more," Candy said, slipping on two oven mittens and pulling out a pan of chicken surrounded by stuffing and little red potatoes.

"Got enough there?" he asked.

"I cook up a big meal then eat leftovers for a week."

He cleared a spot on the counter for her to set the pan. She nodded toward the end of the sink. "That's unoccupied."

He set down the pies he'd picked up. "It's occu*pied* now."

She groaned and handed him two plates, two cups, and two small bowls. "Just for that—" She stuck a rolled-up set of place mats under his arm.

"I'm not inviting myself for dinner," he argued.

"It's a treat to have someone to eat with. Besides, I want to shamelessly pry into your personal life."

As if that was punishment enough to offset the privilege, he grunted his assent.

Candy chopped up some cabbage for coleslaw and sliced a carrot. Things were going rather well, considering the fact that she'd asked him that afternoon never to come back and had whipped up this whole supper just in case he did.

Land sakes, she thought, trying out one of her country expressions. When a woman relived the sensation of a man's hands all over her skin at the oddest moments during the day, when she still felt the heat of their flesh touching and catching fire, when the warmest breeze on her cheek recalled his breath, when even the telephone poles reminded her he was out there working somewhere, she felt justified in learning a little more about him than his name, the location of his parents' farm, and that he hadn't eaten properly. Not since her breakfast.

She turned around to find the table set, Zach poised with a fork in one hand and a knife in the other. "We ready?"

"I thought you'd say yes."

He patted his stomach. "Think I did before you asked."

She draped a linen napkin across her lap, and he hastily followed suit. "This is where you earn your dinner. Tell me about you."

Zach trotted out the small talk. How long had he been a lineman? Fourteen years. How long had he lived there? All his life. How did he like her chicken fricassee?

"Seconds?" He had his plate in his hand and was halfway out of his chair.

"Be my guest."

He dished up another helping and put a tiny wing on her plate before she could object. "Don't know what else to tell you." He concentrated on buttering a biscuit. "Don't know what you've heard."

"Did you imagine me canvassing the community in one day?"

He chewed thoughtfully. "Yeah."

She tossed her napkin on the table with a huff. "And to think I fed you dinner!"

He chuckled and covered her hand with his, aware in an instant of her warmth, the fine bones of her hand, the drift of her perfume subtly threading its way through the cooking smells. Her fingers curled slightly and he ran his thumb across her palm until they curved around him. "Hate to see these get callused."

"I'll be careful."

That could apply to a lot of things. "It's hard, a woman running a farm."

"Grace does it."

"So does my mother, more or less. Ever since Pa went blind."

"I didn't know that, I'm sorry."

"He's been that way a long time. He helps however he can. Some things on a farm you need a man for, women's lib and all."

She smiled and let go of his hand, picking up their plates and carrying them to the sink. "It isn't always a question of ask and you shall receive." She turned on the hot water, gazing out the window at the fading light over the fields. "Maybe I could rent one."

Zach piled the rest of the dishes beside the sink.

"Are you an only child?" she asked out of the blue.

"No."

For some reason that surprised her. There was something very "only" about him.

He answered her questioning look. "I've got an older sister, Jean. I had a brother."

"I'm sorry again," she replied softly.

Zach inhaled deeply, glad the past tense was all he'd needed. "Jean's got a boy, Jesse, almost seventeen. Makes me feel old."

Candy shot him a teasing smile, swirling the water to make the suds grow.

"A heartbreaker. Half the high-school girls trail after him. Got to have a talk with that boy."

"The kindly-uncle type of talk?"

"Jean thought I might get through to him. His dad can't. Don't know where she got this idea I'm some kind of sex expert."

Candy caught him looking at her in the window's reflection. "I'm not saying a word."

Zach laughed and took the plate she handed him, drying it until it squeaked. *Sex expert!* He couldn't tiptoe out of that mine field if he tried. So he stayed quiet, wiping the dishes as they came his way, watching the flicker of a fine gold chain on her wrist dip in and out of the glinting suds. The match for that necklace, he realized. He wanted to ask if she'd have any problem getting it repaired, but . . . Joking about sex was one thing, directly referring to the previous night was another.

Not that he expected it to happen again.

She seemed to sense him looking at her. The silence in the room grew as thick as the steam covering the window. Candy told him a little about her former job in New York, "just a job," she called it. She looked forward to farming, doing something meaningful.

Zach thought of something meaningful. If she lit a fire in the fireplace, invited him out to the living room—that would mean something. It might chase away the idea gnawing at him, that she wanted to pretend the night before hadn't happened, to block out the whole thing, and him with it.

He watched the pile of dishes dwindle to silverware. She ran her fingertips over the bottom of the sink, seeking strays. When she lifted her hands out and shook them, he reached out to dry them with the towel, patting them between both of his.

She smiled an aren't-you-nice, first-date kind of smile. He wanted the firelit one, the one that said thank you for saving my life.

Dishtowel in hand, he deliberately wrapped it around each of her wrists, leaving three or four inches in between to loop the ends and fashion a loose knot.

"Uh, Zach, you've got me, um . . ."

Tied in knots? They were even. He fingered her thin bracelet, pushing it a little higher on her wrist so the towel didn't pinch it. "Sorry I broke that necklace."

"It was an accident. You didn't mean it."

"I didn't mean to break it."

"I can have it fixed. I should have taken it to the jeweler in town today." She went to snap her fingers; the soft cuffs stopped her in mid-gesture. "I'll do it tomorrow, when I take the pies in." She rattled off the names of families on her list, those still without power.

Lips pursed and brow furrowed, Zach nodded as if sagely approving of her plan. Patiently he waited.

For what? Candy wondered, her throat growing dry, her breasts tight. His dark eyes mirrored the darkness that descended outside. She absently plucked at the knot with the tips of her fingers, scanning the room for something else to chat about. What on earth did a woman talk about when a man had her wide-eyed, tongue-tied, and in every other way roped and lassoed?

He didn't scare her. Devilish male smiles had never made her heart skitter for cover. Roller coasters couldn't make a woman's stomach plummet when she was a hundred miles from the nearest amusement park, could they?

He leaned a hand on the sink ledge, his shoulders at an angle, his smile unconsciously imitating their slant. "You're going to do it, aren't you?"

"Do what?"

"Pretend this isn't happening."

"It's a joke."

"Is it?" He hooked a finger over the knot and tugged her toward him. "Candy, I've always believed there are some circumstances when people should never lie to each other. Last night was one of 'em. Tonight's another."

She swallowed. "I thought we settled all this this afternoon."

"So did I."

"We aren't going to be an item. This isn't about sex."

"Not casual sex."

She didn't ask about the other kind. Her voice, strong not strident, assertive without being breathy or in any way seductive, failed her completely. Her tongue turned coward, and her lips betrayed her with every flutter of breath they let pass through. "Zach, what are you doing?"

"Untying you."

Unraveling her was more like it. She felt weak and shivery and suddenly too feminine to stand without wilting. She rebelled at the entire notion of clinging to a man out of sheer erotic delight. But what good did rebellion do if her body had already surrendered?

He slipped the towel free, and her hands felt so lightweight, she had to tug them back to prevent them resting palm flat against his chest.

"I wondered what it would take to get you to acknowledge what's going on here," he said, his voice gritty.

"This is a friendly supper. Last night was a fluke."

"Was it?" He leaned toward her, pausing inches away, waiting for the answer to his question. "Was it, Candy?"

Yes, she wanted to scream. She wanted to clench her teeth and stand her ground and not—repeat not—feel her toes uncurl as the scant distance between them evaporated like the glittering suds in the kitchen sink.

Her throat got as thick as one of the horrible biscuits she'd made him eat. He'd wolfed them down like manna from heaven, then he dared turn around and treat her as even more precious. *Damn you, Zach, for making me want what I can't have.*

She threw her arms around his neck and kissed him. The fool deserved it. He deserved every groan she dragged out of him. He deserved her hands rifling his hair and her knee banging against his, and most of all he deserved to know exactly what torture a man could put a woman through when he made her crave his mouth, his taste, and every emotion that caught fire in the dark—the liquid warmth, the static racing across her skin, the heat suffusing her.

His hands nearly spanned her waist. His thumbs clamped on her and he set her down at last. Breathing hard, he rested his cheek against her forehead. Her moist lips tarried against his throat.

"I didn't plan on doing this," he said hoarsely. "I want you to know that. Until I got here—" He unveiled her ear with a callused palm and placed a kiss beneath her lobe.

She buckled against him and said his name. She felt balanced on a high wire, electrified, so finely strung, she'd break if he touched her once more. . . . And collapse if he didn't.

"Tonight, Candy. It won't be rough. It'll be for you."

The drain chugalugged, giving her conscience a chance to catch up with her galloping senses. "Wait." The word emerged with barely more substance than the bursting bubbles. Yet she knew Zach would honor it. He was a good man, he'd respect her wishes. But which ones? Her desires had suddenly turned dark and uninhibited, submerged in memories of the previous night, surrounded by his arms.

The radio hissed and crackled. The station signed off at sundown. How long had they been standing in the pool of light by the sink? Darkness hemmed them in, waiting for them to join it.

"Zach—" She shook her head, forcing herself to step back. "Last night was for you. That's all it was."

He lifted her chin. "Don't tell me you weren't with me all the way."

She shook her head. "Please. Maybe I wanted last night, too, but that was a once-in-a-lifetime thing."

"Yes it was." He grinned.

"We couldn't recapture it if we tried."

"I wasn't going to try."

"Then maybe we should call a halt to this before it becomes something neither of us planned."

"You want me to go?"

She couldn't lie. She let her hands slip from his. "I think that would be wise."

"If you want wisdom, talk to Grace."

She had half a mind to. Because her new life couldn't include children, she'd thought it wouldn't include men. He was offering her far more than she could ever return. "Here." She picked up a fresh cherry pie and handed it to him. "We'll be friends. I mean that, Zach. If you ever need anybody. If you want anything, anything but—"

He grinned and took the pie out of her hands. "I know what you mean."

Did he? For some reason it tore her apart to see the lonely walls he'd erected rise between them. He looked tired again—life tired.

"And you be *my* friend," she insisted. "I'm all alone out here, Zach. I can use all the friends I can get." She ushered him toward the door, twining her arm through his while making sure her thigh didn't brush against him. She lifted his jacket off a peg. "I won't say we made a mistake or that it didn't happen. It's"—she almost said indelible—"undeniable. It's probably my fault for giving you the wrong impression."

"No way."

"Will you be my friend?"

Through heaven and hell. He stood there while she helped him into his jacket, bobbling the pie pan from one hand to the other as he shrugged on his coat. Crafty woman. She'd tied his hands as efficiently as he'd tied hers.

She leaned over and held the screen door. "You have a nice night now."

"Right." He got one foot onto the porch and gave up. With one long reach he snaked his arm around her shoulders and yanked her to him, kissing her open mouth until cherry pie, apple pie, every kind of pie in the whole wide world took a backseat to the taste of Candy. "Glad we got this straight," he said, dropping her back on her heels and shrugging inside his coat until it set right on his shoulders again. "See you around."

Speechless, she nodded.

He got in his truck and backed all the way down the drive, his arm crooked over the seat as he stared through the back slider. He caught sight of her as he took off down the road. She was standing beneath the yard light they'd repaired that afternoon. It could have been a lifetime ago.

It'd be another lifetime before he'd believe a woman so beautiful, so elegant would settle down to country living. Zach clung to the idea the way a drowning man catches a rope. She'd get bored, she'd leave. That was his only hope.

Repaying debts was one thing, but how did a man repay the good that came his way? He owed her, that much was clear. So he'd "git" when she said "git" and nod when she said "go" and he wouldn't believe a word of it when she called what was between them a friendship.

What was it then? He wondered.

He gripped the steering wheel until the plastic squeaked under his hand. The word *love* clattered around in his brain like gravel in a hubcap. Pulling into his drive, a shooting star caught him making a wayward wish.

"Young, you've got yourself in one hell of a mess."

Five

Candy stood in the hospital corridor for a moment not even sure how she'd gotten there. A wave of temporary relief washed over her; it was a small country hospital, not a noisy, disruptive big-city emergency room. Her every sense had rebelled at the idea of Zach being in such a place. The nurse had left her standing at the counter while she paged the doctor for information, allowing Candy a moment to catch her breath.

Returning, the nurse asked if she was a relative.

"A friend." She'd promised him she'd be that much—she just hadn't expected to live up to it so soon.

She'd been in the high-school gym, serving up pie to the families stranded by the tornado. Casseroles had come in by the dozens. Grace Griddell ladled out soup and ordered the children to take extra napkins.

When the general manager of the electric co-op had arrived as promised to explain how much longer it would take to restore power, the scene had turned ugly. Demands were made, fingers jabbed the air.

"Why don't *we* have priority?"

"Whose lines *are* you putting up?"

"My cousin said she saw a group of them sitting in a truck drinking coffee yesterday."

"They've got to eat too," the general manager had explained, the strain of the last week breaking through. "Don't you ever call my men lazy. Those men are doing all they can, including risking their lives. I've got two men in a hospital right now from burns, one of them in critical condition. No one, and I repeat, no one, is dragging his butt on this!"

A hush had fallen over the room. Candy's ears had buzzed with a rush like a second tornado. If she could have blocked out the next words, she would have; nothing had stopped the quietly spoken names of Tom Warsaw and Zach Young from piercing the roar in her ears.

"Sit down, honey," Grace had said.

She had turned on her companion. "Where would they have taken them?"

Without asking why, Grace had said, "Parker Community General."

Candy had sunk into a cold metal folding chair, her legs suddenly giving way. "He didn't say which one was in critical condition," she'd murmured.

Grace had touched her shoulder. "You won't be any good around here until you know. I'll give you directions."

Staring up and down the two corridors that made up the hospital, the vinyl shiny with disinfectant, Candy tried to compose herself. Was he all right? What had happened? The next question could wait; Why had it been so imperative that she rush to his side?

She closed her eyes and inhaled the sickly-sweet odor of a mop and pail parked beside the row of plastic chairs. A knot lodged in her throat, growing bigger when she spotted a doctor coming down the hallway. She stood, her legs rubbery.

"You're here about Zach Young?"

"I'm just a friend. I only wanted to know if he was all right. I don't have any right—"

"He's chased off everyone else. Maybe you can talk to him. Tell him Tom Warsaw has been upgraded to serious condition at the burn center in Wichita; he's out of danger."

"What about Zach?"

"Second- and third-degree burns on his arm from the entry point to the exit point." The doctor motioned from his palm to his elbow. "Electricity is like a microwave, it burns mostly from the inside. Wherever the electricity exits—you're not going to faint on me, are you?"

Candy realized she'd turned ash white and licked a salty dampness off her lips. "I'll be all right."

The doctor's concerned frown was interrupted by Zach's voice thundering through a doorway. "Dammit, I'm not staying in this damn bed answering a bunch of cockamamie questions—"

The doctor pushed open a door and Candy entered.

She found Zach halfway out of the far side of the bed, another man blocking his way. Zach clenched the back of his gown with a curse when he saw her in the doorway. "Where're my pants?"

Candy straightened her shoulders and walked right up to him, her shoes sticking to the slick floor, her mouth set. Her voice steely, she muttered for his benefit, "Darn you, Zach Young, I know I'm a knockout, but I've never landed a man flat on his back before."

"Very funny." His mouth twitched, but the scowl stayed firmly in place. His forehead featured a gash and a purple bruise no one had the decency to warn her about, his cheeks were drawn, and his eyes rimmed with dark circles. "Have you seen my pants?"

Candy cocked her head to one side. "What would I have to do with your pants?"

He didn't answer that, seeing every person in the room was against him getting out of there. "I'm going home."

"Not if the doctor says no."

"The doctor says no," the doctor replied from the doorway.

Zach spat out an expletive, trapped between Candy on one side, the doctor guarding the door, and Henry Kennedy, the statewide safety director for electric cooperatives. "Henry, you going to help me?"

"Tom Warsaw is in the best of hands, Zach, there's nothing you can do for him by going to Wichita."

"He's been upgraded," Candy said. "The doctor says he's out of danger."

"He would've been out of it quicker if I'd gotten to him faster."

"How long did it take?" Henry asked, clicking lead into his mechanical pencil and taking notes.

Fed up holding his robe closed with his one good hand, Zach finally muttered a string of curses and kicked his feet under the covers. If there was one thing he hated, it was talking. What you *did* mattered, not what you talked about doing.

He stuffed a pillow behind his back. Suddenly he felt Candy's small hand on his shoulder, gently pushing him forward as she fluffed it for him. Dammit, you don't have to be so good to me, he thought. He was in a mood for an argument, for accusations, for name-calling, all of it aimed at him. He wasn't in any mood to be coddled or petted or—

He caught her eye, her flash of a smile as she patted him on the shoulder, wordlessly encouraging him to go on with the story.

She was being *nice*, the cheerful volunteer he'd heard about in town, getting involved when people were down, helping out. He hated the idea of being just another project on her list.

He didn't know why the hell that should bother him, he'd never expected to be anybody's lover. He was too hardened, had been alone too long, had too much experience pushing people away. Then he thought of the one night with her, the way he'd held her, clung to her, their motions rough with need. His need.

Henry Kennedy cleared his throat.

Zach grimaced, taking a long time to exhale. "Tom was up the pole. A primary line had been broken by a tree branch. We tested it, it was dead. Got the limb off it and began hoisting it back up."

It was a clear sunny day. Beautiful. No wind, no clouds. The weather didn't have to be terrible for terrible things to happen. Zach recalled another tragedy on a day as crisp and blue.

"Did you ground it?"

He evaded the answer for a minute. Candy set her hand on the bed. Zach looked at it, looked at her. He would have touched her if he could. He tried to clench his left hand and winced at the pain and the lack of response. "No," he said. "It was wrong, it was lazy, and no, we didn't. The line was dead. People are ripping our heads off for how long it's taking to get their power on, we wanted to get it done and go."

Henry said nothing and wrote.

Zach turned to Candy, his warm brown eyes boring into hers. "It's safety regulations, but half the time you don't follow every blessed rule, especially not when you're in a hurry."

"You were in a hurry?" Henry asked.

"We've been in a hurry for a week, dammit."

"Go on."

Zach couldn't speak, not for a minute. It was his

fault. As crew leader he should have insisted on dotting every *i* and crossing every *t*. Usually he did. But Tom had been a lineman as long as he had. He got huffy if Zach picked on him. After years together Zach knew when to back off.

Cutting corners had almost gotten Tom killed. And Zach could have prevented it.

"Even though the line was dead, Tom wore his gloves just in case." Zach explained the gloves men wore when working with live wires, how they held 7,200 volts of power in their hands, protected by nothing more than heavy rubber. "There must have been a hole in them. With the work load we've been pulling down, you don't get a chance to check 'em after every single job."

Candy's legs turned rubbery all over again, and she pulled up a chair without interrupting the flow of his words.

"The tester alarm went off. All of a sudden the line was energized. Someone must have thrown on a generator, and it was feeding back down the line. Tom yelled down that he'd keep working, then it happened. His body stiffened and he slumped, nothing but his belt holding him to the pole."

The room was so silent, Candy heard a phone purring at the front desk.

Zach said nothing for a minute while the picture of the electrocuted man swayed in each person's imagination.

"The current passed out his boot, you could see the sparks shooting off his spikes."

Candy saw Zach's hand clench and unclench on the sheet. His left hand was heavily wrapped, the bandage stained by some kind of burn salve. She swallowed against a nauseated feeling when she thought of what the doctor had said about electricity burning from the inside. No one would know how badly Tom

Warsaw was hurt until X rays were made. It could have been Zach.

When he didn't speak, Candy touched his shoulder. He nodded and cleared his throat but didn't look at her. His familiar scent cut through the hospital aromas almost painfully, and Candy felt her throat close up with tears.

"I got on my belt and strapped on my spikes and started to climb. I yelled to Jerry to radio for an ambulance."

"Esther says there was some confusion on the radio," Henry commented.

"The kid was flustered, okay? He got the message in." Zach ran his good hand through his hair. A lock fell over his forehead. Candy clutched the edge of the mattress rather than comb it back.

Zach felt her action and looked over at her, his eyes so bleak, she wished she'd touched him.

"Where is Jerry anyway? Is he okay?"

"A couple of men took him out for a drink to settle him down. They'll look after him."

Zach took a deep breath and purposely made his left fingers close, more punishment than exercise. Jerry had freaked, his stutter so bad, he could barely get out the name and number of their truck. Zach had screamed at him from the pole and the kid eventually had gotten the job done. The rest had been up to Zach.

"I climbed up under Tom and got my belt around under his." He'd fashioned a hoist out of the rope winch Tom had been using to raise the line, and had looped it through the man's belt. Then he'd cut Tom's belt with a splicing knife and felt the tug of the unconscious man's weight on the rope. Zach was about to lower him to the ground when Tom suddenly came to.

"He panicked. It happens. He woke up dangling

thirty feet off the ground, in shock, and he struck out."

The wrench clutched in his frozen hand had clipped Zach on the forehead so hard, he'd seen zigzags of light. Forced to grip the rope winch with one hand, he'd fought off the panicking man as they'd swung in midair, live wires slung inches over their heads.

"I don't know how we touched the line. One minute we're wrestling, the next my arm feels like someone set it on fire. The second jolt stunned Tom, and I got him lowered to the ground. Jerry took over then."

Henry nodded. "You two were damn lucky, duking it out under seventy-two hundred volts of hot wire."

Candy put her fingertips to her lips but couldn't hide the horror in her eyes.

"Sorry," Zach said, apologizing for her hearing the story, for everything.

"No," she said, touching him. She had to touch him. "You're going to be all right. Tom is too."

"I should have done more, should've made that mule follow every rule—"

"You followed every one as far as rescues go," Henry said, adding for Candy's benefit, "the dummies we use in practice don't wake up and take a swing at you. Lucky your boyfriend has a hard head."

Zach smiled and stared bleakly at the sheet. "I did what I could, Henry. We'll just have to wait and see if it was enough." He shook his head. "Accidents," he said, a sarcastic edge to his voice. "This sort of thing seems to happen when I'm around."

"It happens," the safety director retorted.

Zach shook his head again. "I could have prevented it—we both know that."

For a moment Candy felt there was something no one was saying, something she didn't know.

"You would've walked through fire for that guy and

we all know it," Henry insisted. "Now get some rest." The doctor ushered him out.

Candy paced to the foot of the bed. "You need your rest."

Zach spoke her name.

Her heart twisted when she caught sight of the ugly egg-sized bump on his forehead, dried blood around the gash. If his elbow hadn't come in contact with the pole, the power wouldn't have exited there. If it had been the toe of his boot, the burn could have traveled through his body like lightning, burning every muscle it coursed through.

"Zach, you did what you could." She came up beside his good arm and took his hand. To her surprise he clutched it tightly in his.

For a minute Zach thought about lifting it to his lips and kissing it. He wanted to taste her, to get the charred taste of blood out of his mouth—he must've bit the inside of his cheek somehow. It wasn't serious. What happened to Tom was. If he'd been paying more attention . . .

"I'm glad you came." He didn't ask why, guessing she'd already prepared some kind of innocuous excuse.

"Zach."

He shook his head, stalling her. He let her hand fall to his lap, working his fingers in between hers so they twined. Then he laid his head back, trying to get the picture of Tom out of his mind, to lessen by sheer force of will the pain shooting through his arm and throbbing in a dizzy orbit around his head.

Her other hand, cool and small against his forehead, gently combed his hair back. He raised the hand he held to his lips and kissed it, holding it against his mouth until she wriggled her fingers. He'd been squeezing too hard. He pulled his mouth away and saw the red pressure mark. "Are you staying?"

"Until they kick me out." She hadn't realized until that moment that she wasn't going anywhere without him. Unable to free her fingers, Candy reached behind her and pulled up a chair. "Hey, you stayed with me when my house was dark and I was alone."

"Here we are with all the lights on surrounded by nurses and doctors and—"

"And strangers."

She looked into his eyes, daring him to say otherwise, challenging him to remember exactly how familiar they'd been with each other, body and soul and fears and needs.

"I'm not that fragile, doll. I've spent nights in hospitals before."

He looked down, his face a mask, as if he'd said more than he intended. Zach rubbed the back of her hand restlessly up and down his thigh and stared out the window. After a minute he said, "You'd think accidents would happen in the rain, the lightning. When you're alert."

"You can't be alert every minute. You don't feel guilty, do you?"

He did, but he wasn't going to wallow in it. He knew what they'd all say—Tom was up, Tom had chosen to go without grounding the pole, and crew leader or not, Zach couldn't very well force the guy to look after his own hide. "Did Henry say they're pouring a few beers down Jerry?"

Candy smiled wryly. "Guess so." She remembered the youngest man of the crew she'd met at her farm. Her farm, she thought suddenly. She was beginning to feel at home there. And here, by Zach.

Watch it, Candy, a warning voice whispered. They were friends, that's why she was with him now.

"He stutters, you know," Zach said.

Candy chuckled. "I remember he had one heck of a time saying hello to me."

"That's because you're pretty."

"Thanks."

He shrugged, realized his whole shoulder hurt, and lifted her hand to his waist. He wondered if she could feel the warmth of him through the hospital gown the way he felt the coolness of her hand.

"Jerry did a good job for a rookie. He radioed it in and helped hold Tom down. Had to practically sit on him until the ambulance got there; he was a wild man."

Candy nodded, wondering with a pang who'd looked after Zach. She suspected he'd downplayed his own injury until someone saw to the wounded crewman.

"What are you thinking?"

She realized she'd been staring in his eyes all this time. "You wouldn't believe me if I told you."

"What?"

"That you're a hero."

He squinched up his face and stared over at the window again.

"Whether you believe it or not."

"Do me a favor," he said.

"Anything."

"Stop by my parents on your way back. My nephew, Jesse, drove 'em here—Ma was too shook up to drive and Pa can't. The kid drives a hundred in school zones. Almost got here before I did."

Candy laughed, her heart swelling when he gave her a pained smile. He lifted her fingers to his lips again. A quiver went through her. "Zach."

His eyes were stormy and dark, his smile wistful and more than a touch sinful. He licked the V between her middle finger and her ring finger.

"You promised we'd stop this," she said, standing when her legs would support her.

"Humor me, I'm sick."

"Ha. You aren't as sick as you look."

"Do I look that bad?"

Her heart hammered a denial. No way she was going to tell him how sexy he looked in a baggy hospital gown with blue and green whales sailing across it. His shoulders and the hard smooth planes of his chest filled it out like a cloth draped over a statue of Michelangelo's *David*. But he was flesh and blood, not marble. Her hero was all too human.

"I noticed you didn't argue when Henry called me your boyfriend."

"It wasn't worth arguing about," she said lightly, "not when there are important things like your being a hero."

"We've been through drills like that a hundred times."

"Glad to see you aren't getting a swelled head. Or are you?" She tapped lightly around the bruise on his forehead.

He caught her hand. This time the heel of her palm received his kiss. Her fingers curled and tiny sparks of electricity shot up and down her arms, making deep parts of her body glow with a languid heat.

He kissed the pulse at her wrist, the faint blue veins climbing her arm. He kissed her the way a marooned sailor kisses the ground of a remote island, bowing his head to land, home.

Her fingers curled around his cheek, stroking gently. If she could just hold him, tell herself he was all right, then go. If she could convince herself he needed her company more than her touch, then her mission was finished.

"Reminds me of old times. Me in bed. You here." His voice rasped.

"We're in a hospital," she whispered. "*You're* in a hospital."

He lay back, lifting his hips to settle in and get comfortable, drawing her eyes that way for a moment, catching them on the way back up with an answering twinkle. "I remember lying on your couch while you talked. You told me a lot that first night."

"I thought you were asleep."

"And I thought I was dreaming."

The woman was real, so was his throb of need, and the unsettling feeling as he looked around the room, that it had been empty until she'd gotten there. For a while it had been filled with people, his parents, doctors, nurses, and too many ghosts from the past. Then she'd walked in.

What was he going to do about her? She was smart enough to tell him to keep his distance. Was he smart enough to listen? People got hurt around him. Accidents, all of them, but he was implicated. His life was filled with debts he'd never repay. How could he take what she offered? Maybe she was being kind, but for him it was rapidly becoming something more.

Woozy, he watched the room spin, then closed his eyes so she wouldn't see how weak he was.

A nurse bustled in with a tray. "You going to help feed him?"

The nurse's blurry voice reached him as if his ears were plugged with cotton. Zach started. He'd fallen asleep. How long? He tried to sit up. Candy squeezed his hand.

"First you eat," the nurse ordered him, "then *you* go."

Candy nodded obediently. "I'll need my hand back to hold this spoon."

Zach let go, knowing he'd be there all night, wrestling with the realization he needed Candy as much as he needed food. Knowing he had no right to ask for anything more.

• • •

On Thursday his mother came into the room, his father gripping her arm. "Checkout day," she announced.

Zach switched off the electric razor and put it in his dad's outstretched hand. "Thanks, Pa."

"You looking presentable? Your mother said you've been letting yourself go in here."

With a pointed look Zach's mother dared him to argue.

"Gotta give the nurses an excuse to pamper me, Pa. You ought to try it sometime. Just lie back and let a woman shave you."

"Your mother'd cut my throat rather than see me babied."

"A grown man ought to take care of himself," Ma insisted.

Zach laughed. The whole family knew his mother would have waited on Pa hand and foot after he went blind. But he'd needed his sense of independence more than maid service.

"And you, you still seeing that New York girl?" Ma asked. "A person would think you'd fix yourself up for her sake instead of looking like one of those scruffy TV detectives."

"I'm not seeing her, Ma, she stops by."

"She stopped by our place," his father said. "Baked us a pie."

Hiding a smile, Zach rubbed his clean-shaven jaw with his good hand. Candy must have a production line of pies coming out of that oven. It was a wonder she didn't open a bakery.

He hauled himself out of bed. "So. I'm staying at your place."

"Till that arm's better."

• • •

Or until he went nuts, Zach decided three days later, pacing his parents' kitchen. He'd agreed to the arrangement to reassure them he was fine. Grumpy maybe, hemmed in, ready to get back to work the next day although his four-week disability was barely a week old.

He'd expected that. What surprised him was the memories that hit him sleeping in his old room, his heels just touching the foot of the maple twin-bed set. Joey's bed stood against the other wall. Nothing ever changed. Nobody let it. They'd kept everything the way it was when Joe died—

"Was killed," Zach muttered as he paced.

His father went in and touched a jacket in the closet. His mother dusted, bustling through it like nothing had changed. Because everything had.

This morning he'd finally noticed.

"What happened to the pictures?"

His mother, scrambling eggs for breakfast, knew what he meant. "We packed them away."

Zach glanced at his father, the old man's head tilted as he listened intently to the morning agricultural report on the radio.

"It was time, Zach," Ma said matter-of-factly.

Zach sat down. Why now? he wondered. Had they cleaned it up for him? Did they think it was time he put it behind him too?

"You got anything planned today?" his mother asked.

"No, Ma. Thought I'd mope around here, sulk in the workshop, maybe waste some time in the barn. You chase me out of here the minute the day-care kids get dropped off."

Pa laughed. "Got some other chores for you, if you'd care to help out."

Zach's shoulders tensed, and he was glad his father couldn't see it. He tried to keep the exasperation out of his voice. "I always help, don't I?"

"I didn't mean us, I meant Jesse."

Zach made an imploring face to his mother. "I tried talking to him about sex, Pa. He thinks he knows it all. That's what 4-H will do to you. Between animal husbandry and Guns n' Roses he could teach me a thing or two."

"Maybe you should let him."

They all laughed, then Zach felt the boom lower. Candy. Somehow they'd maneuvered him around to Candy again. Subtlety he didn't need.

"Why don't you invite that young lady you're seeing to supper sometime?" his mother asked.

"I'm not seeing her." He hadn't worked up the nerve.

She'd visited him every day in the hospital. He'd begun planning his days around her, straining his brain for witty things to say, memorizing articles in the paper he could comment on. When she got there, he forgot it all, just held her hand and stared at her. . . .

He knew he wanted too much from her. He was proud enough to deplore the fact it showed. He had to pull back before she became a necessity and not just a lingering, twenty-four-hour ache.

"Invite her over when you see her," Pa said.

"We could thank her for the pie," his mother said.

He hated when they ganged up on him. "The Team," his sister Jean called them. They were pushing him into this, and he didn't know why. They wanted him married. They wanted him to get over Joey's death. Some things a person didn't get over.

"I don't know when I'll be seeing her, Pa."

"Go out with Jesse."

"What's Jesse got to do with this?"

His mother answered patiently. "He's taking a load of organic fertilizer—"

"Manure—" his father said bluntly.

"Over to her farm, get her planting started. We said you'd help out."

He didn't need to remind them his left arm was in a sling. He had a sinking feeling another part of his anatomy was too. They had him railroaded and he knew it.

"Keep the boy in line," Pa said.

Zach tore the crust off his toast. As if the kid would make a move on Candy. As if any man in this town would dare. The rush of jealousy ambushed him. He set the toast on his plate aside.

Hell, the kid was seventeen years old and drove like a bat out of hell.

He'd probably'd dump half the manure on Candy's front lawn instead of where it was supposed to go.

The woman had a farm to run alone. She had no experience and no man to help out. He owed it to her to help her at least get the fertilizer plowed in properly.

Owing. Repaying. Responsibility. Those were terms Zach understood. In a sense he still owed her for that first night. And for the dinner she'd cooked him, the pie she'd baked, all those visits to the hospital. The debt was mounting; he had to do something to knock it down. "I'll give the kid a call."

Six

Jesse Lamont hopped down from the dilapidated farm truck wearing stovepipe jeans and cowboy boots. The denim, faded and worn until it formed a second skin, emphasized lean and muscled legs and hips narrowed in proportion to the V-shape of his shoulders. He had a face like an angel, a smile to put Don Juan to shame, and eyelashes a camel would cry for.

And he knew it.

"Candy Wharton, I presume?"

Candy bit back a smile and extended her hand to the seventeen-year-old. "Mr. Lamont?"

"Aw, you can call me Jesse."

"As in Jesse James?"

"As in outlaw," Zach grumbled, coming up from the other side of the truck.

"Zach!" Candy went up on tiptoe to kiss him on the cheek.

Zach stiffly bent to receive it. "Candy, this is Jesse, my nephew."

"Candy suits you," the young man said, taking her hand again. "Sweet."

Glancing up at Zach, Candy tried not to roll her eyes. The wattage this kid put out was incredible. But there was a world of difference between men and boys. "How's your arm, Zach?"

"Great. We got your manure."

She laughed and dried her hands on a dishtowel she'd carried into the yard. Zach caught sight of it, recognizing the blue stripes. Candy deftly draped it across her wrist and nodded toward the truck, wrinkling her nose. "As my father says, 'if you've got it, spread it around.' What do I do?"

"Stand back," Zach said.

"Hop on board," Jessee said.

Candy laughed and decided to get involved.

Jesse demonstrated the dump-truck controls, showing off his levers and knobs. Candy acted as interested as she could while Zach shouted orders to the boy, backing him up with hand signals. After they'd finished the unloading and downed a few glasses of lemonade, all three gathered around the old tractor in the barn to attach the implement to groove the fertilizer into the ground.

"Let's see if she starts first," Zach said.

Candy scampered up to the metal seat. With the effortless agility of youth Jesse scampered up after her. He leaned a little too close over her shoulder, pointing out the choke and giving directions. The kid even smelled good, she noticed.

Candy didn't care, she was too busy glancing at Zach bending back the engine cover as the fractious machine chugged to life, smoked diesel fuel, burned oil, and promptly sputtered to a halt.

"Try it again," he yelled.

She hadn't seen him in days, telling herself it was better that way, telling herself they had no obligation to each other, telling herself the man still had one good hand, why the heck couldn't he dial a phone with it?

She yanked on the choke with more force than necessary and the whole contraption shuddered and jerked, roaring to life. Jesse hopped down, fingers hooked in his back pockets, and wandered around the back of the tractor.

"Think that'll do it?" she shouted over the din.

"Ought to," Zach yelled up. "Put it in gear."

The backfire boomed like a cannon.

Zach's head came up fast. He urgently scanned the room for Candy first, then Jesse.

Candy's heart lodged in her throat. A chilled sickness swept over her, and her hands tightened on the steering wheel. She'd seen Zach in the hospital grimly but steadily recounting what had happened to him and Tom Warsaw. She'd never seen him scared—until now. "Zach?"

He leaned one hand on the fender and closed his eyes, expelling a pent-up breath. His jaw clenched so tightly, Candy saw the vein pound. "Zach?"

Without a backward glance he slammed down the engine cover and walked out of the barn.

Candy gently eased in the choke until the engine died of its own accord. "Jesse?"

Jesse glanced up at her, extending a hand to help her down.

"What happened?"

The boy shrugged, staring uneasily after his uncle. "Guess he doesn't like loud noises."

Candy didn't know whether he was joking or not. "Why would that bother him?"

He didn't answer. The dust in the barn flickered and swirled through the light that ribboned in between the cracks in the walls. Dry hay, manure, and diesel fumes mixed, making Candy queasy. For some reason her stomach felt hollow. "Jesse?"

His back to her, the boy stepped into the sun-drenched doorway and pulled a bandanna out of his back pocket, wiping the grease off his hands. "It may have something to do with him killing his brother."

The words were so soft, Candy wasn't sure she'd heard them.

"It was an accident," he continued. "Before I was born. He would've been my uncle Joe, Mom's younger brother, Zach's older one. Maybe *he* ought to tell you."

Candy nodded, her head bobbing on a neck that felt stiff. Like a puppet she made her legs move. She followed Jesse out of the barn, scanning the yard for Zach.

He stood beside the truck, looking out over the fields, his good arm folded over the one in the sling.

Food, Candy thought, her mind suddenly clearing. She veered toward the kitchen. "Jesse, you tell your uncle lunch will be ready in fifteen minutes."

"Why, thank you, Ms. Wharton. But I have to be going. Got a date." He winked.

Candy didn't particularly care. "I've made an entire meal. Tell him that. I'll drive him home afterward, it's just down the road."

"Yeah, I'll tell him." Jesse strode over to the truck, his muffled words halting Zach as he climbed into the cab.

Candy didn't wait to hear his answer; she didn't want to argue. She had a meal to prepare.

Zach caught up to her at the bottom of the porch steps. "Candy, I don't want to impose—"

"I have to write a check for that fertilizer, and Jesse's in a hurry."

Jesse had already started the truck and backed it around so it faced down the drive. He leaned out the open window, his elbow balancing on the sill. "Don't worry about getting him home, Ms. Wharton. He doesn't have a curfew."

Radio blaring, the truck rattled down the drive as Zach stared after it. Candy turned on her heel and tried to flee in a dignified manner.

"I'd hate to see all that food go to waste," she sang out over her shoulder. "I've got enough to feed a dozen hungry farmhands."

"Did you take it in mind to feed this whole county when you moved here?"

"I took it in mind to feed you," she said, chin high. "The least you can do is say yes."

Candy piled carrots and cabbage and tomatoes out of the salad bin and nodded Zach toward the bathroom to wash up. She had to have a moment to think.

Jesse's words echoed like a sonic boom. *Killed his brother.*

That might explain Zach's occasional distance, his moodiness. People in town talked fondly of him but rarely got below the surface.

No one got close to Zach Young. Except Candy, one night, when the world had turned upside down. She'd promised herself ever since she'd cool things down, but she couldn't leave a man in pain. Why had it taken her so long to see he carried around more than just loneliness?

Zach finished washing up and came into the kitchen grumbling good-naturedly. "You always put food in front of me."

She skipped right over his comment. "You know where the chair is, Young. Sit and eat."

He sat.

Candy chatted. She saw the strain around his eyes, the aftershocks of whatever memory had come back to him in the barn. She ached to think he kept it all to himself—that he didn't suspect people saw or knew or cared.

If the man didn't feel like talking, she would. She'd fill him up with words and potatoes and coleslaw and fresh baked bread. She'd slap together cold chicken sandwiches and smooth whatever worries creased the space between his brows.

She'd keep her theories to herself—for now. About how a man might carry a memory around until it stooped his shoulders and dug lines beside his smile. How a man, under certain circumstances, might give and never think to take for himself.

They ate while the radio played lunchtime jazz in the background. Zach complimented her on every course she served. After a while he loosened up and began talking about spark plugs for the tractor, a dozen ways he could tinker with the engine and make it run better for her.

"That's mighty sweet of you." He was a sweet man. A considerate one. He couldn't have done anything—

"You need a hand around here," he said. "Just so happens I have one."

She gave him a wry smile. "It's your only one. Sure you don't want to keep it?"

"Seriously I'd like to help you out. I've got three weeks off, and I don't handle downtime well."

"I think we're peas in a pod, always have to be doing something for somebody." She laughed and poured him some more milk, setting a kettle on the stove.

"What's that for?" he asked.

"Coffee. Later."

He looked at her for a long moment. She took a slow breath and watched him in return. So she was inviting him to stay. She wasn't going to let him fluster her into apologizing for it.

"You're being real good to me," he said.

"I could say the same for you."

"Why?"

"Why so suspicious?"

"Why so generous?"

She found herself hovering by a stove that could take care of itself and made herself sit and face him. "I like you. I respect everything you are and everything you do and have done for me. And for others."

He grumbled and started to get up. "More hero stuff?"

She touched his knee next to the table leg. He stilled. "That night we had together. You've been very good about it. No pressuring me for more."

"Not much. Candy, I don't want you getting the wrong idea."

"That's why I thought it'd be nice for us to sit down and talk like friends. To prove it doesn't have to go any further," she said in a very rational voice.

"What if I want it to? What if it could?"

She shook her head. "I'm coming off a marriage that wasn't perfect. Some of the major faults were mine."

"I find that hard to believe."

"Believe it. And why aren't you married?"

His head came up. She recognized that defensive glint in his eye. "See?" she said. "We're both resolutely single. We could both use the friendship. That's why I appreciate your help with the farm. Very much."

Zach would've appreciated a swift kick in the pants, if one had been available. They were back to the "just friends" routine. Fine. Hadn't he told himself earlier that he ought to stop her from becoming a fixture in his life? Helping her out temporarily was the perfect solution. He'd pay her back for all her kindness and they'd be square.

A friend like Candy Wharton would stick by him a lifetime—she was that kind of woman. As long as he kept his mind, his hormones, and his lower anatomy off the subject of their first night, he'd be okay.

"Do we have a deal?" she asked.

"Run it by me again."

"You help me get this place up and running, I'll fix you dinner, say three nights a week."

"You're gonna fatten me up. Have you always linked caring with food?"

She nodded firmly. "Comes from cooking for my dad after Mom died."

"When was that?" he asked, his voice low but gentle.

"When I was fourteen. She had cancer," Candy added. "We had a long time to get used to the idea she'd be going."

"Must have been hard all the same."

She squeezed his hand in thanks. "We had a lot of help. Dad's the pastor of a church. A lot of women from the congregation came over and helped out. I insisted on cooking. I don't have many other great talents."

"You always look like a million bucks."

"Background."

"Breeding," he teased.

"This isn't the 4-H!" She laughed and shook her head, her hair swaying, a strand whispering over her cheek.

Zach's heart clutched in his chest. He wanted to see her do that again, in slow motion this time. Black hair caressing pink cheeks. Before he could free his good hand, she'd reached up and pulled the strand back.

"I meant social background. The church is in a

very wealthy area; most of my friends had new cars at sixteen. We never had money to match theirs, but the sense of style rubbed off. Values were what mattered most to Mom and Dad."

"They must have been good people."

She nodded. "So I'm not the dilettante you take me for."

"I haven't thought that in a while." The third time she kept her promise to visit him in the hospital, he'd given up hoping she'd skip town. Any woman who'd put up with him carping about hospital food had to have a heart of gold. Knowing where she got it didn't make resisting her any easier.

"Then what *do* you think of me?" she asked. "If I'm not a debutante or a dilettante?"

His voice got so low, it caught a couple times. "I couldn't rightly say what I think. Not to a pastor's daughter."

Candy felt the fire creeping up her cheeks. He enclosed her hand with his fingers, pressing her palm flat to his. Heat, a hint of dampness, a touch of friction, shimmered between his skin and hers.

"I think about you all the time, Candy. I picture us . . ."

His breathing was shallow and short, his chest rising and falling as if he'd just run a long way, not as if he'd been sitting there an hour taking a load off.

"What's so funny?" she asked when his mouth crooked in a private smile. She tried, and failed, to slip her hand out of his.

He wasn't letting go. "Remember what we said, about pretending nothing was happening between us? It is, Candy. You can stay away, I can try. It isn't going to work."

She shook her head, her hair whispering. "No, it won't. None of it will. I can't offer you any more than friendship, Zach."

"So I'm being an insensitive jerk? Refusing to take a hint?"

"That's not it. You know I think the world of you—I mean—"

He scooted forward on his chair, leaning toward her until he felt her breath on his face. He wasn't going to kiss her. He watched her tongue dart out and wet her lips just in case. He smiled again, a hard, determined smile. "It isn't what we've been saying to each other, it's what we've done. Where we've been together."

She was one brave woman, Zach had to hand her that. She looked him in the eye.

He reached up and cupped her cheek, the soft heat of her warming to his words. "Men can lie about stuff like this. I won't lie, Candy. You mean a lot to me."

Something flickered in her eyes, a doubt, a question. "We hardly know each other."

"What's to tell?"

She looked at him, trying to hide the keenness in her eyes that seemed to pin him down.

He pulled back, sat up a bit straighter. He hitched a heel on the crossbar of his chair and rested his bad arm on his knee. The blood coursing through him made it ache. She wanted words.

"Okay. I'm not married. Never have been. There've been some women. I can't make you any grand promises. But we can have more than friendship. I think we're sharing more than that now. I want more."

He sensed his answer didn't satisfy her. "What more can I say?"

She got up and went to the sink.

He cursed silently, his foot hitting the floor. Words and Zach never did get along. He'd rather do. Show. Work at something. He got up and followed her.

She scraped scraps into a garbage pail, a butter

knife clicking against the plate. He came up behind her, let his thighs nudge hers, his hips mold behind hers. She paused.

"Zach, please don't."

He roped his arm around her waist and pulled her gently into him. He felt her relax, succumb, her back against his chest, her hips against his hardness, her softly rounded stomach under his palm. He pressed lightly. She covered his hand with hers.

"Please."

"Please what?" he whispered against her hair.

She blindly fumbled the plate into the sink, the knife clattering after, and turned in his arms. She bumped his bad arm. He winced. "Sorry."

He shook his head as if it didn't matter. "Please what?"

The man could make that question sound like an invitation to heaven.

"Don't fall in love with me, Zach. Please. I can be there for you as a friend, but I can't be more. I can't be a wife. I can't be a mother."

He chuckled, and she raised her gaze from the second button on his plaid shirt. "I wasn't asking you to be the mother of my children. That's what these are for." He made a move to reach for his back pocket and his wallet.

Candy flushed three shades of pink, each darker than the last, and shoved him away. She slung an apron over her head and reached behind her to tie the knot. Her trembling hands complicated matters. He tugged on the finished bow the minute she completed it, undoing everything she'd been trying to accomplish. "Zach!"

He had the temerity to laugh when she snapped at him. "You wouldn't hit a one-armed man, would you?"

"Don't tempt me."

"Get thee behind me, Satan?" He insinuated himself behind her at the sink, doing things only a devil would dare.

"You're going to hurt that arm."

"But everything else is going to feel so much better."

She ran the water so hot, steam rose around them. "Get out of there."

He was nuzzling her ear. He knew she loved it when he did that. The fiend. "Cut it out."

"Uh-uh."

"Zach Young, you have always been a gentleman."

"Until now."

She turned and faced him down as well as she could while bent back against a rapidly filling sink. "You're hurt."

"It'll hurt worse if we don't do something about it. Believe me, I know. The nurse at the hospital even commented on it."

"She didn't!"

"I couldn't help it. You'd come to visit. I'd go to sleep thinking about you. Next thing you know, it was morning and there she was, trying to swing that tray into position over the bed."

"You don't mean to say—"

He grinned. "She said this can be some pretty powerful medicine." She'd actually said love was powerful medicine, it gave a man a reason to heal fast.

"You mean to say you have compromised me from here to Parker General?"

"And it all started right there on your couch."

"That's where it's going to end!"

"Is it?"

"No! I mean, yes! I mean—back off."

He staggered back. The woman had more shove in her than he gave her credit for. She swung around and snapped off the faucets, the water nearly sloshing over as she tossed in dishes. "Are you going to help or are you going to stand there?"

"At attention."

She almost glanced down but caught herself in time. Her eyes narrowed to slits of black. "You have a filthy mind, Zachary Young."

"I manage."

"How could you even begin to think such things with your arm in a sling?"

"Come on, Candy. You have more imagination than that." He joined her at the sink. "We both know it."

She would never, repeat never, live down that night. The man would not let her. This was her punishment. "You're exactly what I deserve, getting carried away the way I did with a stranger."

"I'm not a stranger now. Were we ever?"

She didn't answer, scrubbing a pan with steel wool until every last bit of grime came off.

"Candy, don't treat me like one."

The steel wool scratched and scraped in the silence that followed. Her hands were too wet to turn the radio on. She listened to his tense breathing and the echo of pleading in his voice. "Zach—"

The kettle on the stove whistled.

She jumped.

Zach crossed and turned it off.

"I know you don't want this turning into sex all the time."

"In my wildest dreams," she said.

"You dream about it too?"

She dried her hands, her heart finally slowed to a reasonable enough beat that she could talk to him like a mature woman. "We needed that night. We needed—each other. Comfort. Contact. Something." Someone. For her it was him, it might always be him.

"Zach, neither one of us wants to debase what we shared and neither is prepared to look at long-term commitments. I know I'm not."

"I agree with you there. But sex doesn't have to be debasing. Not if a man cares about a woman. Shows her he does." He touched her again.

If she died a little inside, it was the sweetest death imaginable. "I can't think when you touch me."

He let his hand fall, skimming the side of her arm as he did so, a callus catching the silk of her blouse. He took his wrist out of the sling and opened his arms. He didn't have to ask. After a second's hesitation she stepped into them.

She wrapped her arms around his waist and felt his chin rest on the top of her head. It felt too good, holding him, listening to his heartbeat beneath her ear. "What am I going to do with you?" she said with a moan.

"You want suggestions?"

She laughed. "No!"

When he spoke again, his voice was unexpectedly hoarse. "I'm as scared as you, especially when it comes to making promises I can't keep. But don't give up on me yet. Let's see where this leads."

She was astounded to find she had to wipe away a tear before she could look at him. She pressed the side of her cheek to his chest again. "I swear, you get my hormones in such an uproar."

He lifted her chin with his thumb. "How about some coffee in front of the fireplace? You pour, I'll start the fire."

She nodded and managed a smile.

Not bad for a woman who felt like an utter failure. What was she going to do with him? If she didn't know better, if she didn't have a willpower of iron, she'd suspect she'd already fallen in love with him.

She couldn't. It would be selfish in the extreme.

After the flush of passion and first love faded, she'd never be the woman he needed. He needed a home. She knew that every time he walked into her kitchen, took a deep breath, and sat himself down as if a meal was a privilege confined to the most fortunate in the world.

To make a home he'd need a wife.

To fill a home he'd need children.

Spooning out more freeze-dried coffee into the cups than absolutely necessary, Candy fortified herself by drinking it strong and black. She sweetened his with sugar and milk. "You need more than I can give, Zach Young. I will not cheat you of that."

But the selfish part of her bargained for what it could get. Tonight, other nights.

She listened to the crackle of the fire starting in the other room, the iron squeak of Zach jerking the flue several times to make sure it was open. Men.

Candy still hadn't asked Grace Griddell how a woman coped without one. She would. She had to. Those were the cards life had dealt her. When you couldn't love for a lifetime, you loved while you could. And you let go with dignity when the time came.

If loving someone meant putting their happiness first, she loved Zach. She wanted him happy, healthy, untroubled, and not alone. She wanted more for him than she could ever give.

To know where to start, to help him heal, she had to find out about his brother. Then she'd let him go.

She shrugged and picked up the tray. She'd have the rest of her life to mend her broken heart.

"You weren't planning on using it again anyway," she murmured wryly.

Mid-afternoon was a strange time for a fire, but the manure delivery ensured every door and window be shut tight, and the house was cool and damp as a consequence.

Setting the tray on the floor beside the sofa, Candy accidentally sloshed hot water on her hand. "Ouch."

Zach kissed it. "Better?"

"Did the nurses at Parker General teach you that?"

He grinned. "Jealous, huh?"

"How do I know? You were there day and night. Dreaming who knows what."

"Getting drafts up my backside."

She laughed. "And you looked so cute in that gown."

"You would have too." He gulped down his coffee so his free arm could wind around her shoulders.

"Does your brain ever rise above your waist, Mr. Young?"

"Just 'cause I like picturing you—"

"—in the *Kama Sutra*."

"I imagine what you're doing during the day. Working on your farm. Helping out in town."

A peculiar pang caught her by surprise. "Really?"

"I picture you back in New York."

"Trying to get rid of me?"

"I meant before. Tell me what you looked like in high school."

She laughed and settled in to reminisce, subtly undermining any romantic notions he might have. "In high school? Pudgy. I'd pay good money for negatives of any photos taken of me then."

"And college?"

"I blossomed, as Dad put it. Slimmed down. Got a degree. Got a job. Got married. Got divorced."

"No, kids."

"No kids. Would you like some pie?"

His hand cupped her shoulder before she could jump up. "Not after that mountain of mashed potatoes."

"You didn't like them?"

"I loved 'em. That's why I can't eat any pie. Normally a man works up an appetite farming, but I haven't done enough lately to work this off."

Drawing her legs under her, she turned to him on the sofa. "What was it like? Growing up on a farm?"

"Busy. Everyone has chores."

"Mm-hmm."

"Ever since I can remember, I've had one job or another. Just look at Jess. He drove a tractor when he was ten."

"Isn't that dangerous?"

"Very. But boys see Dad doin' it and want to too. You have to supervise them."

She nodded, and they stared into the fire. "Was it a tractor accident?" she asked quietly.

Zach didn't move. His good arm rested around her shoulders, his bandaged hand palm up on his leg. And yet he managed to become more still. It was as if the fire itself ceased flickering in his eyes. "Did Jesse say something?"

"He said you had a brother. You told me that." She laid her hand on his leg. The muscle jerked. Part of her knew he hadn't meant it intentionally. She retreated anyway. "I'm sorry if my asking—"

"You would've heard it eventually."

"Do you want to talk about it?" Had he ever? she wondered. Zach wouldn't impose his suffering on anyone.

He scowled at the fire. Why was it every time he sat on this couch with this woman, he did things, felt things, reached for things he hadn't dared to in twenty years? And why should it hurt so much to sense them slipping out of his grasp?

A tired voice answered from deep inside him: because some things you couldn't change. Like the fact that you'd killed your brother.

He rested both elbows on his knees. The exit wound hurt like hell, but at least it was a clear explainable pain. Unlike the throb near his heart.

He'd found a refuge there with Candy, a sanctuary, a home where no one blamed him or pitied him or forgave him. Where he could be like any other man who wanted a woman. Someone who wasn't locked into a cycle of atonement, making paybacks for something no one could ever set a price on.

The pain seared through him like a lightning bolt. He pressed down on his elbow but couldn't blot it out. A deeper pain flared in his chest, familiar as an old wound.

"Was it an accident?" she asked softly.

"I shot him. I shot him in the back."

Seven

Candy couldn't breathe. She stared at the fire and waited for the world to move again.

Zack spoke. "I was fourteen. He was seventeen, going off to college that fall. We were out hunting in the woods, coming back from Commencement Creek. Me, Pa, and Joey. It was a beautiful day. Beautiful day. Blue sky, the cornstalks gold, crackling as we walked through a field."

He cleared his throat and looked at the floor between his knees. "I tripped on some rusted wire somebody'd left at the end of a cornrow. Dropped my gun."

"It went off?"

"I yelled but—Pa turned around so fast he caught Joey as he fell. We were miles from the nearest house. We couldn't move him. Pa held him until he died. Then he carried him all the way to the Jackson ranch. My father was a very strong man in those days."

Candy covered her mouth and swallowed a moan.

"He went blind within the year. Something about

watching his oldest son die. The doctors didn't say that, but that's what it was."

"Then it's psychosomatic?"

"It's just as real."

"I'm sorry, I didn't mean—"

He shook his head. "I know. I've been through all the excuses. Hating myself, blaming myself, wishing I could go back in time and live it over. Wishing it had been me instead."

"Don't say that."

He didn't argue. "After a while you get on with your life. I worked the farm, trying to replace Joe *and* Pa. Got a good job to bring in more money. I can't complain."

No, Candy thought, he never would. Zack wasn't one to ask for help. Now she knew why. She put her arms around him, glad he didn't tense, aware it took him some effort not to.

He let her hold him. Then he patted her arm. "I've been through the pity too."

She stiffened. Her breath caught.

Clumsy, he turned inside the loose circle of her arms as she began to pull away and reached around her waist, hauling her to his chest with his one good hand. "I'm sorry," he said, pressing a rough kiss to her hair. "I didn't mean to hurt you."

He touched her face, running his bandaged thumb over her lips. They looked swollen. Kisses should give them that soft look not unshed tears. "You're good to me."

Candy couldn't say anything. Emotions clogged her throat until it ached. She laid her cheek against his shoulder and held him for a moment. "Zach, I'm so sorry."

"It was a long time ago."

"Does that make any difference?" Who had held him all this time? Who'd ever gotten close enough?

Because of one night and one storm, she had. How swiftly a person's life could change. An accident had haunted Zach for twenty years. An accident had brought them together. Maybe it could help him heal.

He squeezed her shoulder. "I ought to be going."

She unwound one arm from his neck and stroked back his hair. He had that guarded look again, the man outside the jewelry-store window. She suddenly pictured Zach as a young man, a gangly boy standing a few feet away from his father and his dying brother, not knowing what to do, knowing there was nothing he could do.

Her eyes filled with tears.

"Hey," he said, a smile tipping the corner of his mouth. "Don't do that." He leaned toward her and touched her lips with his so sweetly, she almost cried out.

She shook her head, blinking away the tears. "That's not pity."

"No?"

It's love, she wanted to say. *I love you, and I wish I'd been there to tell you years ago.*

He kissed her again, a farewell kiss. She felt his muscles tense as if to rise. She gripped the front of his shirt. He wasn't walking away, not now. She flattened her palm to his chest, holding it over his heart, feeling the beat imperceptibly speed up.

His mouth opened. Her heart stopped. She leaned forward to kiss him. Boldly, she let the tip of her tongue touch his. An electric current sizzled through her. Their first time had been fire and lightning and thunder rumbling down from the heavens. Suddenly his touch lanced through her, an intimacy that laid bare everything, demanding everything a woman could give.

She'd been naked with him before, by firelight and

stormlight. She'd taken him into her body, held him to her heart. This time he needed more. "Don't leave," she whispered, her lips tingling as she separated them from his.

"I'll have to. Eventually."

That's when she knew he meant forever. Her heart plummeted. "Why?"

He looked away as if searching for the words. "Because I can't come here pretending it didn't happen."

"Is that what you've been doing? Pretending?"

His eyes got hard, a flash of anger glinting in them. He shook his head. "You should know better than that." He gripped her to him so hard, the breath rushed out of her. He parted her lips with no warning, no request, just need and the harsh facts of life. His tongue pierced her, his hands tangling in her hair until her head fell back and he scraped her neck with kisses.

Finished, he tore himself away from her. "Before today I could come here and pretend none of it happened. That this was another place and I wasn't a killer. I did one of the worst things a man can do, Candy."

"It was an accident."

"That doesn't change it. That first night here, you didn't know anything about me. I liked that. With you I could be another man. We could talk, flirt, make love. Be like everybody else."

She didn't know when she'd started fumbling with the buttons on his shirt, somewhere in the heat of the moment, in the tussling and grappling. The only thing that seemed to matter was getting through, finding skin, tasting it. Until he shook his head no.

"I killed my brother."

She took his face in her hands. "Zach Young, don't you dare tell me you're going to let the past run your life. You're braver than that. You're not hiding, not here or anywhere. Not anymore. And never with me."

She practically unhinged a vertebra in his neck when she forced his head into an up-and-down nod. He would've smiled, but something inside him hurt too much.

Hiding was exactly what he'd been doing. Leave it to her to see right through him.

That first night had shown him something he hadn't even realized, something that had hounded him most of his life. It was time to put the past behind him, to sit in a kitchen with a woman, to go to bed with one. To seize love when he found it.

He couldn't hide anymore. And dammit, he didn't want to.

His voice came out harsh and quick. "I want you."

And she was there.

His hands were all over her, his mouth plundering hers with no finesse. His lower body surged against his constricting jeans. If he could have caught her hand and pressed it against him, he would have.

But his good hand was snarled in her hair, the other useless and clumsy inside its bandages. Getting her undressed wasn't going to be easy. Neither was convincing her he wanted more than sex—he wanted it all.

It felt like breaking through a wall, like hard chunks of earth cleaved by a plow and turned over in the sun—he wanted to live again, and Candy was the reason.

It was as real as the quiet snick of a bra being unhooked, the rasp of denim under his hand as he cupped her rear end and urged her onto his lap. "Candy."

She made a little gasping sound, then a knowing moan, the sound of a woman's voice when she can't find the words but knows the sensations all too well.

He cupped her breast with his palm, toyed with the pebbled peak of the other, but her blouse— "I'll be damned if I can get these buttons undone with one hand, babe."

She'd finished with his shirt, tugging the tails from his jeans. "Next?" she asked silkily, beginning with her top button and working her way down.

His mouth got dry. He drank from hers.

She rocked back, peeling her blouse off her shoulders and letting it fall. Her hand rested on the top button of her jeans. She raised a brow in invitation. "Next?"

He glanced past her at the bedroom door. "How about taking me in there first?"

Her eyes darkened, that mysterious black that could twinkle or smolder or fill with tears for him. Not this time. Her lids lowered and she studied his mouth, his chin, her fingertip making an indentation there like a dimple. Then she traced a path past his Adam's apple, across his collarbone, through his chest hair, straight to his belt buckle. He sucked in his breath and felt her slip her fingers into his waistband.

"The bedroom then." She led him, her hand playfully tugging his belt.

"I'll go after this," he offered.

"You'll stay," she quietly commanded him.

His mouth twisted in a smile. Candy Wharton had more heart than was good for her. He'd have to protect her from that as firmly as he'd protected her from learning about his past. Reluctant as he was to color what they had with bad blood and outstanding debts, none of it fazed her. She was there for him, without question. Just the way she'd been that first night.

He flicked on the light switch out of habit. The

overhead fixture made no difference in the glimmering afternoon light. She didn't seem to notice or care. Their hands bumped as they both closed the door. She leaned her back against it.

"I've imagined you here."

He smiled. That voice of hers, smooth as a polished stone, turned him to jelly. "How many times?"

"How many nights have there been?"

He splayed his palm on the door beside her head, pressing it flat when she turned her head and skimmed a kiss up his wrist. His voice came out crusty. "What happened to the 'just-friends' stuff?"

"I meant that. When I said it."

He laughed low. "Shows you what good words are." He ran his bandaged fingers down her open blouse. "Mind if we don't talk right now?"

She pulled off her headband and tossed it across the room. It landed on a hat rack beside the mirror.

"Bull's-eye," he said. The word died on his lips as he turned.

She ran both her hands through her hair, black strands untwining. Her breasts rode high and firm, her shirt filmy and fluttering on either side of their soft swells. "Kiss me," she said.

He complied. They swayed as he lifted her away from the door.

Candy knew his strength. At times it had impressed, intimidated, and aroused her, like the night when he'd so deftly tied her hands. But it was the way he carried off her heart that worried her. His commitment to those things that mattered to him was tenacious and fierce.

Wounds took a long time to heal in such a man.

His love would last a lifetime.

He unzipped her jeans. She quivered. A scattering of tiny black hairs on her lower abdomen caught his attention. His touch made her knees weak. He swung his arm in its sling back and forth, skimming her tender skin with his bare fingertips.

Knowing he couldn't do more with that hand, she slid her own down, slipping it inside the part of her jeans, the lace trim of her panties. Easing both down, she stepped out of them. Then she reached up and lifted the sling over his head.

"No fair," she murmured. "You're wearing more than I am."

"Not for long."

She stood on her tiptoes and kissed him. "I love you," she whispered.

He swallowed but didn't speak.

"Make love to me," she asked with no hesitation, no fear, no pity. "I need you."

"Are you undressing me?" he asked, glancing at her busy hands.

"What do you think? You can't do it with your arm in a sling."

"You're about to find out what I can do."

Candy gave him a soft shove, prodding him back toward the bed until he sat. She hauled off his boots. He took care of the socks.

Candy busied herself with folding down the sheets and spread, then settled herself beside him to unbuckle his belt.

He still blamed himself for the accident. Any woman with eyes could see that. She had to show him what was plain as day; despite everything, the man deserved love, a woman, a home, and a family. When he believed that as surely as she did, she'd let him go and find them.

But first she had to convince him. To do that she'd love him like no woman ever had.

He tipped up her chin. "You're frowning."

"This buttonhole on your waistband is frayed. Every time I get the button out, it catches."

He reached in with his thumb and forefinger and simply snapped the offending threads. "Try the zipper," he said. He stood, like an oak growing in the middle of her bedroom.

Her throat grew dry. "Sit down again."

"It'll be easier to get them off this way."

The golden light flooding in the window behind him couldn't have been more different from the stormy night that brought them together. Outside all was gentleness and peace; the true storm raged inside.

Candy shivered as he hooked his good hand in the waistband on the right side, directing her to tug on the other. The jeans came off in one motion. He wore nothing beneath them.

Candy blushed. That the absence of underwear should make her heart palpitate was downright adolescent.

There was nothing adolescent about the man before her. He stepped up against her, rubbing her softly rounded stomach with his satiny shaft. She melted like butter inside. The room grew warmer.

"Stay here," he murmured when she would have backed up. His fingers skittered down her lower back, the peachy hair on her thigh. He kneaded her with one hand and felt her muscles tense.

"Relax," he whispered, his mouth beside her ear. His hand spanned her again, one finger straying to a curlicue of hair, damp and slick between her legs. "Tight can be good too."

Her knees went weak. "I'm sorry."

"What for?"

She'd meant to be the strong one, to give without inhibition, to show him how much love he deserved. "I'm quaking like an expectant virgin." She caught sight of his grin out of the corner of her eyes as they fluttered open.

"Don't you think I like that? Candy, you make me harder than—" He didn't finish the thought, too busy nibbling her shoulder.

"But I wanted to show you how much—"

"You are."

She hoped so, her senses muddied by the swirling feather-light sensation. Logic couldn't penetrate the fog of anticipation and lassitude, the heaviness that made her want to sink onto the bed and lazily discover what other delights Zach Young had mastered. But the torpor in her limbs disappeared like an evaporating mirage when she imagined his weight, the melding of their bodies.

"You're not afraid, are you?" he asked in between kisses, when he knew darn well she couldn't form any coherent defense.

She shook her head. He probably thought that meant she loved the way he fondled her breast, taking the way her hair shimmied across her shoulders as a sign to nip them again. She was vulnerable. As vulnerable as she'd ever been with a man. If that wasn't a time to be afraid, she didn't know what was.

The first time had been needs of all kinds, clashing on a stormy night. The challenge was making love to a man she cared for so much but couldn't keep.

She put her hands on his shoulders to steady herself. "This wasn't supposed to be about me. This is for you."

"Because you feel sorry for me?"

"No."

"You want me?"

"Oh yes."

"Know what I want?"

"What?" she whispered.

"To have fun."

"Fun?" The word sounded as foreign as *afraid*.

He let her go suddenly, turning to yank down the

bedspread with his bad hand. He hid a flinch. That quickly he knew he couldn't very well sweep her off her feet with one arm. He hoisted her over his shoulder in a fireman's lift instead, depositing her flat on her back in the middle of the bed.

"Zach!"

"You rang?"

He stretched over her, laughing as she relocated a dozen throw pillows from underneath her. Her body rolled and pitched as he angled over it. "Caught between a hard and a soft place?" he asked.

The hard place became apparent. She stopped wriggling.

"Pillows everywhere." He scowled, relegating a few more to the floor with a sweep of his hand. "And the softest spot in the house right here."

She gasped as he touched her.

He kissed her navel, those fine black hairs, the line her panties left. "What's the name of that perfume?"

"Obsession," she replied when he looked up at her.

"You always wear it down here? Or did you put that on for me?"

She nodded so he'd know for sure.

"Then wear it only for me," he demanded.

She nodded again. Any woman could put on perfume for a man. Some other woman could give him even more than that. *After* Candy had finished loving him. "Be careful of your arm."

"I'll take care of it."

"I want to take care of you."

"How?" he dared.

She pushed him slowly over on his back. "You're the one who doesn't like words. Let me show you."

She proceeded to do just that, teasing him with her hands, stroking and caressing until he clutched her wrist and breathed her name. She raised her head from the nipple she'd been tormenting and smiled her slyest smile. "Give up?"

"Up is the word."

She chuckled.

"You coming with me?"

She nodded.

"Then come here."

Edging up on her knees, she mounted him slowly, filling herself with the taut heat of him. She bent forward, skimming her breasts across him, capturing his mouth. His hands gripped her waist and urged her down, beginning a rhythm that built quickly.

He watched her eyelids flickering, her tongue darting out to wet her lips. He felt her hips clench and ease. His breathing got ragged, his body ready. "Candy, babe."

"I want you on me. I want to feel you."

He watched her move on him, catching her rhythm and taking her higher. "Next time."

She nodded, her neck arching, her back, her thighs gripping as she slid down on him, rocking faster, her abdomen rippling with the motion.

The back of his hand grazed her full breast, her downy stomach.

She'd never felt so naked, so new. His gaze was steady and even. A light sheen of effort shone on the line of his jaw as answering desire built in him. She felt him move faster, meeting her motion with his, and rejoiced. A sensation like something igniting exploded in waves coursing through her and she raced it to the peak, her head thrown back, her body shuddering. Only Zach's hands, firm and strong, held her to the earth, to him.

He got her beneath him, working out a way to lean on his right arm without crushing her completely. She didn't seem to mind. Not judging by the way she said his name, the way she hooked her legs around his hips and welcomed him into her.

They'd lain quietly for a while after the first time. Curled on his chest, Candy had held him inside her as long as she dared. Minutes had gone by, maybe an hour. The light sank lower but days such as this never really ended. That she knew. Days such as this you kept in your heart. And men such as him you held on to.

He pinched her bottom.

"Oh!" She slapped his hand. "Devil."

"The Devil in Ms. Wharton. What would your father think of that?"

"I'm a grown woman, he doesn't ask."

A pang of guilt cut through Candy. Not the predictable kind. She guessed what her father's opinion would be if he ever met Zach Young. "He's a good man, keep him," Dad would say, probably before he was done shaking his hand.

"Where're you going?" Zach asked.

"Bathroom," she whispered.

"Be back soon."

She tripped away, only to find him flagrantly decked out on the bed when she returned. He slouched his shoulders against the headboard, three or four of her throw pillows clustered behind his lower back. His bad arm was canted over his head. Slanting light outlined every muscle and ripple of his body.

He opened his sleepy eyes. Barely. "Something funny?"

His husky growl might make a less secure woman tremble to her toes. Noting the quiver in her limbs, Candy decided she wasn't as sure of herself as she'd thought. She plopped down on the bed beside him anyway, running a hand down the slope of his narrow waist.

Ticklish, he twitched.

"I was thinking you looked like a painting," she said. "Apollo and Daphne or Adonis. Or Narcissus by the pool."

He grinned.

"Definitely Narcissus."

"Must be the light," he grumbled.

"Must be," she said lightly, planting a soft kiss on his lips. "I don't get too many Greek gods in bed."

His arm snaked out lazily, tumbling her across his waist. His eyes were stormy and just turbulent enough to start something. "You aren't getting any more of 'em either. Not if I have anything to say about it."

"Jealous?"

"Smart enough to hold on to something great."

"Threatening to cast a lightning bolt my way?"

"I think I just did." He stroked her thigh until tiny reminders of the electricity they generated slithered under her skin.

"Now, what can I do for you?"

Zach groaned. As if she had to ask.

Eight

He got her beneath him. He loved the way he felt inside her. Electric, like a current humming and sparking, the peaks getting higher and higher.

Among the pillows and the covers this time, careful about how much weight his other elbow would take and how much her body willingly would, he tried to reach the floor.

"What?" she asked, eyes glazed with desire.

"Need my wallet," he said. The wrapper of the last condom lay discarded by the end table, but he had more.

She murmured something he didn't hear. It sounded like no.

He loved where he was. It felt great, unsheathed, slick, the slight friction when she clenched around him, but, dammit, he was only a man. If they didn't take a break now, it'd be too late.

He smoothed the hair off her face and kissed her long and hard, hoping for a second to distract himself from the throbbing urgency of their union. A man showed how much he loved a woman by taking care of her—looking out for unwanted pregnancies was one of the first ways. "Candy, wait."

He'd all but stopped, yet she insisted on making little insinuating motions with her hips. Lord love an eager woman.

"Honey, don't do that. Candy!" His voice came out a little louder than he'd have liked.

Her eyes flashed open. "What?"

"Hold on a minute. I need to put one of these on." *If* he could reach them. "Hand me my wallet, will you?"

Guilt cut through her as she glanced down. "We don't really need one."

"No?"

"Not if you don't have any infectious diseases," she said lightly. She'd been through enough doctors and tests in the last two years to know.

"You sure?"

She reached out an arm and twined it around his, pulling his arm back in, meshing their fingers in evocative poses until she pressed his palm to her breast. She shook her head. "No need."

"The rhythm method's a little chancy—"

"Don't you like this?"

A dry laugh escaped him, although any movement at all threatened to undo him. "Hon, this is as good as it gets. Don't let any man tell you different." He rested his forehead on hers a moment, planting a light kiss on her temple. "Without that latex—" He couldn't describe it. Every sensation instantly received, topping the one before with jolts of pure pleasure. How did a man tell a woman that?

He breathed a devout thank you. "We've got to stop or else."

She pulled him closer. The effort of holding himself just so made his right biceps quiver. So did her touch. "Don't stop now. Please, Zach. Give me this."

Emotions he couldn't name buffeted him. That she'd even consider having a child with him . . . Days ago he'd barely let thoughts of a future with a woman taunt him. There he was suddenly taking a chance on a whole new life, not just his own, but the one they might create.

Zach thrust slowly inside her. A moan escaped him. She had a faraway smile on her face, a sad smile. He kissed it away. "I love you," he said. And he loved every gift she'd given him, including this unlooked-for faith in the two of them. Deep in his heart he promised her he'd never forget that.

He moved faster. Every sight, sound, and smell in the room burned into his mind—the flannel sheets, the heat of her body, the catch of her inarticulate cries, the whisper of her hair, her perfume, their joining—all the promises that entailed.

"I've gotta move—my arm," he said, rolling off her.

She nodded, little aftershocks coursing through her. She stroked his arm. "You didn't hurt yourself, did you?"

"The only way I could have hurt myself," he said, "would be if we'd gone on another three or four hours."

Candy laughed, cursing herself inside for making the biggest mistake of her life. Oh, she'd been such a fool! To think she could make love with him without loving him even more.

When he'd asked about condoms, she'd made an idiotic remark about him not having any infectious diseases. She'd forgotten passion could be infectious, like a flash flood on a country road, sweeping you from your moorings.

And desire. A woman could catch the desire shining in a man's eyes like thunderclouds on the horizon, heedless of the warning boom of a heartbeat.

And joy. Damn it all to hell, nothing was more contagious than joy. It positively burst from him when he held her close.

He loved her. He'd said it and he'd showed it. Why did it have to hurt so much?

She knew the answer—because love and trust, though slower to grow, were as infectious as any of the above. Once touched by them, Candy couldn't keep them to herself. Her trust for Zach grew deeper the longer she knew him.

She'd made a terrible mistake. The idea had been to convince him any woman could love him, not just one. If he fell in love with her, it might not be so easy to extricate him from the promises he'd made in the heat of passion, from his sense of duty.

From his happiness.

Lying there, listening to his quiet chuckle, she was terribly afraid she'd weep.

"What is it?" His smile remained for a moment, an afterimage at odds with his instant concern. "Candy?"

Fighting it every step of the way, she felt her eyes brim with tears. She wrapped her arms around his neck and pulled him to her; it was easier to hide that way.

He snatched his injured arm out of the way before it got caught between their bodies, barely restraining a yelp of pain. "Careful. Candy. What is it?"

"Nothing."

"No, it isn't."

"Haven't you ever had a woman burst into tears after making love?"

"Can't say I have. This is good?"

Her body quaked under his, and she managed a laugh, her chest bumping his as she sniffed. She hauled a corner of sheet up from under him and wiped her nose daintily. "I wanted to do more."

He got very still. "That wasn't enough?"

"For you."

"Did you hear me complaining?"

"When you touch me, having you inside me . . ." She had to sniff again, deploring the way her eyes puffed up when she cried, deploring the fact that she wasn't making any sense at all. "I'm making a fool of myself, I know." How did you explain to a man that he really shouldn't love you, not if he knew what was good for him?

He shook his head, his worry fading to a wry grin. "You can run me through more emotions than a semi has gears, you know that? Just tell me I didn't hurt you somehow."

"I'm fine. I just—I wanted to do so much for you, and every time you touched me I'd forget all of it."

He threw his head back and laughed out loud. "That was kind of the idea. You know how that makes a man feel, having a woman respond so eagerly?"

When she smiled, the tears leaked out the crinkles beside her eyes. "I'm glad you're happy."

"I was a little surprised, that's all. After all my lectures to Jess on birth control. Here we are—"

"Oh, that." She turned her head on the pillow he'd retrieved for her and looked around the room, at his sling tossed across a wicker chair, her headband on the hat rack, his shirt draped over the footboard. "Just don't be *too* happy, okay?"

"Superstitious?"

She almost nodded. "Realistic. This can't last, Zach. Not forever."

"Who's to say?"

"I am. Please." She reached for him again. "Just hold me. This'll pass, I know it will."

As if she referred to nothing but the sudden storm of tears, he silently did as she asked, tenderly wrapping her in his arms as her body shook. "I'm here. As long as you need me."

That could be a very long time, Candy thought, the tears flowing unchecked.

During the next two weeks he stopped by every day. She wouldn't let him stay overnight, using every argument in her arsenal to get that fact across. What would his parents think? The neighbors, distant though they might be, couldn't miss his truck parked outside. He needed rest, not work around her place. She picked every nit.

He countered them all.

And every evening, after the day's work was done, prices compared on replacement equipment, irrigation schemes laid out, sections of the farm divided off for the various plantings, they retired to the house for dinner.

And every night he touched her and she came to him.

Some nights she struggled with her own desire, others she slipped into the circle of his arms, the halo of firelight, the sheets on the bed, and they made love. It had to be. Like air, like water, like the steady light from the bedside lamp.

Whether tender, fierce, or fun, when it was over Zach got dressed and left, because that's what she said she wanted.

Candy wanted to strangle the man. Her wants were entirely beside the point! She was supposed to be making him happy and whole, to make him see he deserved more than he'd let himself have. That he could forgive himself and be loved.

"How do you convince a man of anything while lying naked in his arms, crying your eyes out?" she asked herself Friday morning, staring out the kitchen window at the road, waiting for the rooster tail of dust that signaled his truck.

"Crying jags, excess emotion. Rampant hormones. Nothing but early-onset PMS," she chided herself. She cried because he was so precious to her, because what they had couldn't last, because a fraction of the joy they might have had tormented her. If only fate and biology hadn't—

"Stop it, Can. He can't be yours."

She loved him too much to tie him down.

Last night she'd done it again, the tears seeping out, matting her lashes. Sexy, he called it, adding that he never wanted her to cry alone. "You come to me," he'd said.

"Okay," she'd lied.

"If you need a shoulder—"

"You've got two big ones." She squeezed them, then hugged him fiercely. Like a friend seeing someone off at a bus depot.

Standing in the kitchen the next morning, she wrapped her arms around her waist and held on tight. Why did it have to feel so good to hold a man?

The events of the last evening lingered in her mind, on her body. He'd parted her thighs with his, had pressed sweetly against her until she'd welcomed him yet again. The tears had subsided, replaced by a quivery breathless anticipation that shimmered just under her skin then sank deeper, like a well plunged into the earth to bring up drenching, life-sustaining water.

"I don't deserve you," she repeated to the empty room and the light of day.

If she didn't tell him the truth soon, it would be too true. She had to let him go, to convince him it was in *his* interest to leave.

His truck turned in the end of the drive.

She'd tell him.

"But not today," she whispered, bargaining with the sunshine, the fields, the wide empty sky. Watching the long lean man hopping down from the truck, his jeans faded and pale, his face tanned and lined, a ready smile curving his lips. "Not yet."

"Zachary Young, I make the purchases, I write the checks, I say who I buy seedlings from and who I don't." Candy didn't wait to be handed up into Zach's truck. She stamped one foot on the step and hauled her behind onto the vinyl seat.

She knew his truck well enough by now to automatically avoid the tear in the seat by scooting over. Habit now, she tugged twice on the shoulder belt and it released. "The whole idea of this expedition was to introduce me to suppliers, not scare them off for good."

"Granted. But those sticks with leaves he sold you aren't fit for a rabbit patch much less a commercial farm. He was ripping you off."

"Because I'm a woman?"

"Because you're a city girl."

"I could have told him I know something about farming."

"You've *read* some things. Out here people might smile and shake your hand, but they'll sell you second rate if they can and excuse it by saying they gotta make a living."

"Then let *me* take him on next time."

Zach grumbled something to himself about taking him on with a good heavy stick. To think that low-baller had tried to cheat Candy.

He started up the engine and scowled all the way out of Wichita. Rumbling down the ruler-straight county road, he steered for a minute with his knee as he switched on the radio with his good hand.

"Does your hand still hurt?"

Zach placed the left one on the wheel, curling his fingers as best he could. "Better every day." If they didn't hit a rut, so the steering wheel kicked back and hit him smack on the entry wound, he'd be fine.

He had one more week on disability before he returned to the electric co-op. He wanted her farm squared away before then. "Look, I know you want to do this on your own. To prove you can."

Candy gave a ladylike snort. "I *know* I can. But I'm not so insecure I can't accept a little help. I appreciate all you're doing, Zach." She touched his forearm as he shifted gears.

He'd have been happier if she'd touched his thigh.

"But," she continued, "you dragging me all over the tri-counties setting me up with suppliers is one thing. What I object to is your hogging the conversation the minute we walk in. It's as if—"

He felt the back of his neck prickling and prepared himself for a feminist lecture he probably deserved. "As if what?"

"As if it's *your* farm," she concluded.

That one brought him up short. That farm was part of her. Taking care of it was just another way of looking after her, of showing her how he felt. He knew how to care for a farm—he was still learning when it came to a woman.

"Maybe I do," he admitted slowly, casting a sidelong glance her way. "Maybe it's time we dealt with that."

He wheeled the truck onto the gravel shoulder. Fence posts and power poles marched to the horizon. The rumble of tractors preparing the land in the fields all around them set up a faint vibration under the unmoving wheels. A haze of dust followed each tractor. Despite the wet spring they needed rain.

Zach and Candy needed to talk.

He reached across the seat back and wiped a strand of hair off her cheek. The window was down. No matter what the temperature, she claimed the scents of farm country were vastly superior to the city. She looked tussled and windblown, her cheeks bright pink and her eyes cautious, very cautious.

"I want to be there for you," he said. "That means Wichita, that means here."

She caught his hand. "You are. You're a great friend." She gripped it when he cursed and tried to pull it away. "I mean that. I'll always be there for you, too, Zach."

"Let me stay the night." It was a simple request. Maybe he could work his way up from evenings to whole nights. Then he'd move some clothes to her place, stay for days at a time. He'd waited this long for the right woman to come along, he didn't have a problem earning a place in her life. It was a new idea, working for something you wanted, instead of paying off something you owed.

"I told you," she said, "I won't live with you. And I don't have any plans to marry again."

It would've worked better if she'd said it to him instead of the dashboard.

"I think we should talk about it," he said, his voice husky.

"Why?"

He squirmed and stared at the road. She would force him to put it into words. "Because of what we've been doing and what we haven't been using. Every now and then, if you're absolutely sure, we can skip the protection, but it's becoming a habit, and if anything happens, I want you to know I'd stick around."

She shook her head, still avoiding his eyes.

"I can understand, Can—hell, I prefer it, it's great without but—worries about pregnancy can inhibit a man as well as a woman."

"*You're* inhibited?" she asked archly.

They both chuckled. Not for long. Soon Candy was staring out the window again, watching a tiny tractor in the distance digging furrows in the ground, burrowing like an ant preparing for winter.

Zach tried again. "If I got a woman pregnant because I was thinking with my belt buckle, I'd never be able to look Jesse in the eye again."

"Mr. Bad Example."

"You said it. I owe the kid. I'm the only uncle he's got."

Candy heard the echoes of the past in his voice and banished them. "You're a great uncle, Zach. And a good man."

And she was the wrong woman for him. She had to draw limits, for both of them. Had to think of a way of encouraging him to leave. She rubbed her forehead, finding it unnecessary to feign a headache. A perfectly good one throbbed right between her eyes. "I think I'll renege on our deal tonight. Your parents haven't seen you for supper for days, and I'm sure your mother wouldn't mind if you got home before midnight for a change."

He watched her for a long moment. "If you want to get pregnant, Candy—"

She shook her head, determined to keep the tears at bay. This time she had no sexual release to blame them on. "Is that what *you* want, Zach? To have children?"

If she could have looked at him, she might have elicited an answer. But on this one subject she felt like a complete and total coward. The silence dragged on.

She reached over and switched on the radio. Nothing. He turned the key a notch and the twang of a pedal steel guitar rang out.

"Drop me off at the farm, okay?"

He started the truck and did as she asked. But that didn't stop him following her into the kitchen. For once he wasn't taking a hint.

"Look at the time!" she exclaimed, her eyes darting to the clock above the stove. Scuttling around the room, she threw dinner together so fast, a person would think she had a cab waiting.

"Coffee for me, thanks," Zach said, stewing. What'd he say wrong? Was he pushing it too far too fast? A few unprotected encounters, and he was practically planning their family. "Okay, so we don't talk about birth control if it embarrasses you."

She began half a dozen sentences; none of them came out right. "I think," she finally began, "that what we have is wonderful. I think you're wonderful."

"And I love you too," he said softly, a fine edge of caution cutting through his words.

Candy felt the closeness and caring of the last three weeks turn as brittle as frost on a blade of grass. She hated to see things end. "Zach, I don't want you falling in love with me."

"You've got a funny way of showing it."

"What we've had was incredible. I thank you for that." She rose up on her toes and kissed him. He didn't bend to receive it. Late-in-the-day razor stubble stung her tender lips. "I don't want you thinking this is a permanent arrangement."

He knew people from New York were sophisticated, but her upbringing, her whole manner belied easy bed partners. "Are you suggesting an affair?"

"You're too good a person to settle for that."

"I could say the same for you."

She tossed one too many scoops of coffee in the coffee maker. Zach didn't mention it. He had a gut feeling he'd need it as strong and black as the night they met.

She scraped the sugar canister across the counter. "Maybe that's the point. You don't really know me, do you?"

"Then tell me."

"Zach, I hate the idea of losing you. I really do. That's why I want us to be friends. For life. For as long as I live here, I won't be able to pass a power station, a yellow truck, or get an electric bill without thinking of you. I couldn't bear for us to end as enemies."

"No," he said flatly, gratified by the startled look in her eyes when he closed in on her. "None of this 'friends' garbage. We can't back up. Not us. Not after what we've done. You had me coming inside you last night. And the night before that. Friends don't do that, Candy. Men and women do when they mean something to each other, when they're willing to risk a hell of a lot more commitment and one heckuva long future together."

Struggling for control, he released her, shafts of pain rippling up his left arm. It felt better than his heart or the sudden vacuum in his lungs. "Candy, I can understand running scared. A lot of people need to back off when things get too close. But this isn't the way to do it. Don't freeze me out."

"It's not your fault, Zach."

He ran a hand through his hair. "Where've I heard that before?"

She gave him such a bereft look, he hauled her into his arms. "Hon, I'm saying this all wrong. I love you."

"I know," she said, choking on a sob.

"I only wanted to talk about the birth control 'cause if you didn't want a baby—hell, if you do, just say so. Which is it?"

She nodded, her eyes brimming.

"We can do that too." He smiled, touching her cheek with his, her mouth with his.

Her lips skimmed softly back and forth against his as she shook her head. "We can't."

"Candy, we make babies or we don't."

"We can't." She shrugged out of his embrace and turned away. The tears she'd expected evaporated. Her eyes were as dry as her throat. Her heart shriveled. "I can't have children, Zach. That's why my marriage ended. That's why I came here. I can't and I won't get married again. I won't put you through that. You deserve more."

The heels of his boots seemed rooted to the floor, as if she'd opened an abyss between them and he could no more reach across three feet than three hundred. "That's why we don't need anything," he said.

She nodded. "No chance."

Hell, this was a kitchen in Kansas, not the Grand Canyon. He took one step forward and put his hands on her waist. Frowning, he ran his palm over the soft mound of her stomach, the two precious orbs of her breasts. "Guess I won't have to share these with any rug rats."

The joke fell flat. She tried to smile. He might as well have handed her a paring knife and let her have a go at his heart for all the good it did.

"I love you, Can. For twenty years I thought I'd never have what we have. If we never have anything but barn cats and field mice running around this place, I'd still consider myself the luckiest man on earth."

She stepped back, the better to gaze up into his eyes, puppy-dog brown and just as sincere.

"Marry me, Candy."

She almost slapped him.

Nine

"Don't you dare, Zach. I will not have understanding.
I will not have sympathy. And by God I will not have
pity!"

He managed a thin smile, but the determination in
his eyes shone like dull steel. "I meant what I said."

"I know you did. That's why I hate it! Can't you see
I'm trying to get rid of you?"

For a second she almost did. He backed up. The
better to stand his ground. "It's going to be harder
than that."

"I can't have children, Zach. I've been tested and
tested and asked the most personal questions you
can imagine. We kept journals on when, how long,
and in what positions. I didn't come all this way to
hoodwink some decent, loving, wonderful man into
thinking he wants to marry me."

"You want to spend your life alone?"

"That's exactly what I want."

"Then we've got a problem. Because I plan on
spending mine with you."

She shook her head, waves of black hair cascading
back and forth. "I won't let you."

"Isn't that up to me?"

"You deserve children. You'd be a great father. I've seen the way you are with Jesse."

"Some things aren't meant to be."

"But you change what you can. We can make sure we don't fall in love any more than we—than you have already. Over that we have some control."

"Except that you can't control how I feel."

"Then you'd better," she said firmly. "I have no intention of marrying you, Zach."

He was about to say "We'll see," but he kept it to himself. Candy in a temper wasn't something he felt comfortable taking on just yet. He was only now learning what real love was. How to prove to a woman she was a damn fool took more subtlety than he'd mastered.

He edged around the kitchen, taking down two mugs without being asked, meeting her at the coffee maker as she got ready to pour. He was right—the stuff was black as river-bottom mud. By the time she added enough cream to lighten hers, it almost overflowed.

He ran his tongue along the rim of his mug, blowing steam off it. "And if I promised I didn't want kids?"

"Promises are words, Zach. People change their minds. Eventually they want more." She looked him in the eye at last. "Nobody likes to settle."

His eyes flashed. He worked his mouth until his jaw ached. He wanted to strike out at anyone who'd imply Candy was second rate—and found himself handcuffed by the fact it was Candy herself.

She spooned more sugar in her mug, tossed a teaspoon in his for good measure, and stirred until a whirlpool formed. "First you wanted me for a night, then a few more."

"That's natural enough."

"I know. Now you want to move in, to marry me. The demands pile up, Zach. It would be children next."

"I can live without children. Not without you," he wanted to shout. But her next words left him stony.

"That's what Jeff said."

"I'm not him."

"No. You're better. That's why I won't let you do the 'honorable' thing and marry me. Maybe we should end it now."

And maybe he should plant his kiester on a kitchen chair and argue her out of it. She couldn't physically eject him. He scraped the ladderback chair across the old linoleum and sat. "Tell me about him."

"Jeff? He's history."

"Funny, I could've sworn he had a hold on you right now."

She rubbed her forehead.

Zach steeled himself. Perhaps because he'd never hoped for love, he'd never realized how ruthless he could be when someone threatened to take it away from him. "This'll hurt you more than me, but I have a right to hear it. Especially if I'm being compared to some jerk I don't even know."

She laughed and set her hand on the chair kitty-corner from him. Lightly she skimmed her fingers across it as if checking for dust, then, cowardly, she chose the chair opposite him. She couldn't settle there either.

"Tell you what. While that casserole's reheating, why don't you wash your hands? We can eat and talk."

Food again. Zach gave her the time she needed to work up to her tale by ambling up from the table and heading for the bathroom. He stopped beside her first, his sore hand resting on her shoulder. "Help me get these bandages off?"

She looked up, startled. Zach never asked for help. Maybe because he knew she wouldn't be able to deny him if he did.

Standing over the sink minutes later, Candy gingerly slipped the narrow end of the scissors between bandage and skin.

"This is going to look ugly," he warned.

She shrugged, careful to confine that motion to her shoulders and not her hands. "One more snip."

A half-moon of dirty bandage peeled off, dropping into the wastebasket. Zach set a box of gauze on the sink ledge. "Why don't you look away."

Candy gave him a wry smile. "Think I'm squeamish?"

"I am. If you turn the least bit green, I'll pass out."

Sure, she thought, and I'm Mother Teresa. But she gave him his privacy, knowing as well as he did it was the pain he wanted to conceal from her. So typical. And so lovable.

From now on they'd never be so easy with each other again, never so emotionally close. Telling him about her infertility had cleared the air somehow, scaled a barrier between them. But that barrier would have to rise again.

She would miss fussing over him. She'd miss a lot of things.

Zach turned off the water and grabbed a towel. "I told you not to look."

She glanced up, holding his gaze for a moment. "Sorry. I didn't see anything." *Except the man I love.*

"It looks a lot worse than it is."

Minimizing his pain for her sake, Candy thought. "I'm sure it'll heal just fine. All the work you've been doing around here can't help."

To her immense relief he refused to take the bait.

"The doctor says I have to exercise it so it doesn't seize up. Therapy." To prove the point he slapped a square of gauze over the entry wound and flexed his fist around it.

Candy watched the vein in his jaw stand out instead of the superficial ease with which he moved his fingers. "Right."

"You don't believe me?"

He asked it so softly, she wouldn't have heard him if they hadn't stood inches apart.

He closed the gap, his kiss tender. She'd wanted rough. He wasn't making this easy for her. She had to be tougher. "I don't think we should."

"I do."

"I won't let you cheat yourself of children."

"I will."

"Stop it."

He couldn't. Her lips were too sweet. There, in the kitchen, in the bedroom, or out on the edge of a field, he wanted her to know she was his. To be dizzy on it, crazy with it. To want and need the way he did.

But Zach wasn't the only one willing to play dirty. When he leaned his hips against the sink and sidled her up his front, easily, familiarly, rubbing himself against her abdomen so he could *prove* he wanted her, she grasped his hand. The bad hand.

He clamped his mouth shut so fast, he almost bit off his tongue.

"Oops," she said.

He stared at her hard. "That hurt."

"Sorry." She dragged him around by the arm until he faced the sink again. "You stand right here, and I'll wrap it for you." She tumbled the box of gauze into the sink, trying to open it and hang on to him at the same time. As if afraid of what he'd get up to if his hand were free.

Zach rested his front against the sink. The cool of the porcelain slowly seeped through his jeans to take the edge off. So did her competent, motherly touch. "You're good at taking care of me."

She smiled. "Remember, I took care of my dad after Mom died. Though he never really needed this." She started the bandage, going around and around until the original square was secure and covered. She tore the end and split it down the middle. "You want the knot palm side up or back side?"

He told her, trying to come up with something clever about "tying the knot." By the time it came to him, she'd wrapped it up and skedaddled back to the kitchen.

Unfair! The word practically bounced off the kitchen walls as Candy yanked the casserole dish out of the oven. Unfair for him to come along, to want to be part of her life. She was too needy, too vulnerable, and far from home.

It *was* her home. Or it would have been, if only she'd had a few more months to get a crop in, to become more like Grace Griddell, self-sufficient, resigned. A woman could live fine without a man.

That's why it was so unfair that love should feel so good. Why should having a man paying attention to your every move, your every emotion, have to feel so tremendous? Why did that swirl of sexual awareness have to start just because he looked at her? Why, why, why?

She cranked on the radio and ran smack into a country-and-western song of the most heartbroken kind. She hadn't sunk into a funk of self-pity and general railing at fate for months. Not since the divorce.

She was fated not to have children. Not to mope about it. And not to have Zach Young.

And yet, her back to the door, she knew the

moment he walked in. His step had become as much a part of her house as the hum of the refrigerator or the squeak of the weather vane on the barn.

His low voice murmured across the room. "You ready to talk about it?"

She spooned out tuna casserole onto two plates and motioned him to sit. "Nothing fancy tonight, I'm afraid."

"Looks great to me. Smells great too."

"Look at the food when you say that." She smiled.

"Should I?"

A little corkscrew of heat winnowed through her. She tore open a bag of potato chips and festooned their plates with them. "The potato course."

"Want to talk?"

About Jeff, he meant. She nodded. It was harder to work up to than she'd imagined. So she plunged in. Facing facts had become a specialty. "Jeff and I were married for five years. The last three years were spent trying for children. He'd wanted to get established first."

She shot Zach a glance. For once he made it easy on her, confining his attention to his plate.

"I take it he blamed you," he said.

"Not at all. He immediately suggested tests. He believed any problem could be solved if you found the right expert and paid him enough."

"And when that didn't work?"

She didn't answer.

Zach's voice was soft but strong, brooking no more hesitations. "Did he walk out on you?"

She didn't miss the way he clenched his knife. "No." She kept her chin raised. "He wanted children, that's normal enough. So I offered to let him go."

"And he went."

"He stayed."

"And?"

"He said we could try for one more year."

"He *gave* you a year?" Zach growled incredulously.

"He didn't have to."

"Nothing like working under a deadline."

"Zach."

"Sorry."

"When it became clear nothing was going to work, I filed the papers, and he agreed not to contest it."

"Huh." Zach crushed a potato chip in his fist and sprinkled the crumbs on his casserole. "You make it sound easy. Marriage involves more than babymaking."

She shrugged. "By the time we remembered there was more to it than that, the rest had withered away. Whatever we originally had . . . I call it the iceberg theory. The ten percent of discontent you sense on the surface can hide ninety-percent coldness underneath."

And like an iceberg she hadn't seen it coming until it had hit her, so convinced she was doing the right thing in letting Jeff go. How noble! What an idiot she'd felt like when she'd discovered he'd gotten another woman pregnant, three months before the final decree. He'd wasted very little time proving he wasn't the failure.

"I've got a chipper I'd like to introduce him to," Zach said, referring to the machine they used to shred tree branches when they trimmed near power lines.

Candy would've laughed, but her throat had turned to paste. She drained her water glass dry. "He's remarried now. They have a baby girl."

"How are *you*?"

"Couldn't be better." She dug in with a gusto, focusing on all her uneaten food. Being a good girl and cleaning off her plate. Doing what was best for

Zach. For Jeff. Thinking of others first. Being a caring person.

Being a sap, she thought, stabbing a forkful of noodles.

"I came out here to start a farm, Zach. I can do it. The rest of this—it's caught me as much by surprise as you. That doesn't mean we're written in the stars or that we have to follow through on this. We hit it off—"

"I'll say."

"—and I let it go too far. For both our sakes don't you think we should cool it down?"

Zach didn't know how she managed to be so all-fired calm. He just knew he resented it like hell. Those potato chips were cutting his insides to ribbons. His little flexing exercise in the bathroom had his hand throbbing like a disco beat. His body wanted her as much as ever, but it was his heart that ran the show. And his heart refused to cooperate.

It pounded in his chest like a bull in a barn stall, stamping and huffing and getting nowhere. How could he argue her out of it? Obviously the ex wasn't the bad guy Zach wanted him to be. Or else Candy was taking all the blame on herself.

Zach knew blame. He'd lived with it a long time.

Before he could speak, Candy jumped up. "Can I get you any more?"

He lifted his coffee cup.

She poured.

He held her wrist until she set down the pot then turned her hand over in his. "You're a very caring person, Candy."

"I try."

"Very nurturing. A man likes that. This man does."

He watched her swallow.

"Just don't call me motherly." She laughed, a slight catch in her voice.

"I'm not the only one who gets along with Jesse."

"That scamp's been standing around flirting while you do all the work."

"I saw him."

"Then you know."

Zach's heart turned over at her serious expression. "Know what?"

She gave him a saucy wink. "Jesse and I have fallen in love and plan to run off together."

Zach released her wrist so he could swat her behind as she snatched up the coffeepot and went back to the stove.

"Wouldn't surprise me a bit," he mumbled.

"But it would break the hearts of all the girls trailing after him. Some women have no pride whatsoever."

And some had more than was good for them, Zach thought. At least she could kid about it. Unless the kidding was another form of defense. He'd have to get around that, around all of it, before he could convince her he loved her. He'd tried showing her. He'd tried telling her. What more could a man do?

Just keep loving her, scout. Something's gotta give.

The next morning he showed up to help out. Not bright, not particularly early, but there. Just the way he planned to be every day for the rest of their lives.

"Right on time," Candy sang out, practically running onto the side porch to give him a friendly smooch.

He held her arms to keep her from hurtling them both off the steps. "You got some guy stashed in there you don't want me to know about?"

"Nope. I've got plans."

So did he. But his started, and all too often ended,

with kissing her until her eyes got that starry sheen and her cheeks flushed with fire.

She punctuated his searching good-morning kiss with a peck on the cheek. "We're going into town."

"Which one?"

"Thayer. We're going to do some shopping. If you want to join me, that is."

"Anytime. Anywhere. Say the word."

She laughed gaily and, neglecting to lock the house door, strode to his truck, her purse swaying as she walked.

"What's in town?" he asked as they pulled into a parking space in front of the hardware store.

"People."

"Coulda told you that at Backbridge Farm."

She beamed at him. She loved it when he called the farm by its name. He didn't have the heart to tell her most folks still called it the Preminger place, for the farmer who owned it years before the Harkers bought it and started their ill-fated vegetable business.

"What kind of people?" he asked.

She looped her arm through his and led him a merry dance down Cavanaugh Street, nodding and howdying everybody they passed. In the canned-fruits aisle of Growers Grocery he finally got her alone long enough to interrogate her. "You want to tell me what's going on, Wharton?"

"We're buying food."

"Candy."

"We're being seen."

"I can see that. Any particular reason you want the whole town to know about us? Last night you all but called this off."

She confronted him, the basket on her arm colliding with his stomach. "So why'd you show up to-day?"

"For the same reason I kissed you last night at the backdoor until your knees buckled and you practically begged me to stay." In his struggle to keep them to a whisper, the last words ground out husky and low.

Candy colored as if he'd shouted it from the bandbox in Veterans' Park. "That wasn't fair."

"Love never is. I happen to believe doing means more than saying. There's a lot of things I want to do with you, Candy. If you'd let me."

"I'm doing today," she stated. "We're letting every woman in town know you're available."

"I'm with *you*."

"That can change. When it does, the ladies around here will know you've come out of hiding. You're on the market, so to speak."

Following her to the meat counter, Zach frowned. "Run that by me again?"

"I want everyone to see what a pleasant, handsome, *willing* man you are."

"If they see that, we'll both be thrown in jail for indecent exposure."

"Mind your manners, young man."

Zach whirled around at the sharp woman's voice behind him.

"Hi, Ma." He dutifully bent for a kiss on the cheek.

"How are you, Candace, dear?"

"Fine, Mrs. Young." Candy gave his mother a hug.

To Zach's astonishment she accepted it without so much as a flinch. None of his family hugged and kissed at the drop of a hat. Emotions came from inside a person, and generally that's where they stayed.

"Will you be attending the annual meeting at Prairieland this weekend?" his mother asked.

Candy hooked an arm through Zach's. "We plan to."

That was the first time he'd heard about it.

His mother patted him on the arm consolingly. "See you there," she said.

The game was up. Zach was being manipulated in ways he hadn't even suspected. Despite Candy's insistence he wait right beside her in the checkout line, he curtly refused. Listening to Candy chat up every single woman in the county, while tactfully showing off his unmarried status, turned his spine to spaghetti.

"Single and *willing*," he muttered, sulking outside by his truck, gnawing a peppermint toothpick he'd found in his glove box. The women in this town had known for years not to get too close to Zach Young. Dates, fine. A kiss good night, maybe. More than that even, as long as they understood the rules up front. Emotionally he only went so far.

Did *he* brag about it when he found the world's greatest, hottest woman in a darkened farmhouse just this side of Commencement Creek? Hell, no. So what right did she have parading him all over town?

It was as if she had radar, zeroing in on any single woman spotted a hundred yards down the sidewalk. He remembered those slabs of beef on display in the meat section of Growers and knew exactly how they felt.

When he came out of the hardware store, she'd piled the groceries in the back of the truck. He slid over an old tire to prevent them from falling down.

"I was wondering where you'd run off to," she said lightly.

He pulled his purchase out of the bag, holding the orange "For Sale" sign to his chest. "Why don't you just put my phone number here and see how many calls I get?"

She covered her mouth and smothered a whoop of laughter.

Zach wasn't laughing. He bore down on her, towering over her until his shadow blotted out the sun. "You think you'll get rid of me that way?"

"Zach, be reasonable."

Reasonable? He was madder'n hell. If she thought—

Then it hit him. He knew exactly what she thought and what she was trying to do. That meant he could end-run her. He could head her off at the pass. He could stymie this little game of hers.

But how?

He had more experience holding women at a distance than holding on to one. He ushered her into the truck. She let him take her arm and observe all the gentlemanly amenities. Only because she wanted the rest of the town to see it.

"Step down a minute, hon."

Candy raised her brows slightly and did as asked.

He wrapped an arm around her waist and clenched her to him, full front, kissing her until he was harder and hotter than he had any right to be in the middle of Cavanaugh Street on a Wednesday morning. "Okay. Get in."

With that he blithely ignored her stunned look and strode to the far side to start up the truck. "Happy?"

"Fine," she replied, hiding her breathlessness by fidgeting with her hair, her jeans, her blouse.

Zach smiled grimly and headed toward Backbridge Farm. Two could play at this game.

But it wasn't a game. The closer they got to her farm, the less secure he felt. He might use her own plot to brand her his for everyone to see, but there was no getting around the fact that she was setting him up for a fall. He hated the ashy taste in his mouth. "You gonna do this publicly?"

"What?"

"Dump me. So every woman in town will know."

"Zach."

"What did you have in mind? Come up onstage at the annual meeting and announce it?"

"I wouldn't. I wouldn't hurt you," she added softly, chastened by his bitter tone.

"You don't want me."

"If we're going to argue, maybe you should just drop me off."

"All right." He swung the truck onto a rutted road, fighting the steering wheel as they hit a string of washed-out gullies on either side of the hump of grass down the middle.

"Where are we going?"

"A place I know. We're going to talk. Any objections?"

Candy fought tendrils of uneasiness. The road led into a patch of woods and a series of low hills, miles off the main track. Finally Zach pulled to a halt beside a dilapidated old cabin on the edge of a river she realized was a branch of Commencement Creek.

"Zach, I don't want to hurt you. Only to make you see we have no future. You'll find someone else."

"You want to hand me off to some other woman, huh?"

"I want what's best for you."

He turned to her, draping one arm over the steering wheel and cutting the engine until all the silence of Kansas crowded up around the windows. "Correct me if I'm wrong, but that sounds like love to me."

Ten

"Tell me I'm wrong."

"Zach, there are tons of other women out there. Everywhere you look. Except you don't."

"Don't need to," he said softly, winding a strand of her hair around his index finger.

"Jesse could haul them in in the dump truck and tumble them onto your lawn."

"I like the one I tumbled myself."

With a huff she unwound her hair and hopped down from the truck, parting the long overgrown grass with her short boots, pacing the foundations of the weathered clapboard building, the unpainted wood worn to gray. A half-dozen rusted beer cans littered a blackened pit where someone had been cooking out beside the front stoop. Twenty yards away bushes and sumac crowded the bank where the creek rippled, flowing fast and agitated despite the dry spell.

"You said last night you never thought you'd have something like this," she reminded Zach quietly. "You can. You just have to find the right woman.

She's out there, Zach, I know she is." *And I've never envied anyone more in my life.*

Candy turned and discovered she was alone. Zach stood down by the riverbank staring at the water, his fists shoved in the pockets of his leather jacket. Maybe he had heard her.

"There isn't one perfect person for each of us, Zach."

Even as she said it she prayed it was true. If it wasn't, she'd just let her one true love get away. That would make two lonely people in the world.

Something flared inside her, stronger than love, possessiveness, protectiveness. She wouldn't let him be hurt—not even by her. She wouldn't let him be lonely. She'd find him a better woman, one who'd make him happy, who'd appreciate his gently teasing manner and the tender-rough way he kissed.

Then she'd hand him over.

And curl up and die.

When he turned, she couldn't avert her gaze. His look pinned her there beside him.

"I love *you,* Candy. You want me to settle for less?"

She shook her head and choked down the lump in her throat. "That's precisely why I'm letting you go."

Zach cursed their impasse. What could he say after "I love you"? What could he do? He'd watched over her, helped her out, stood by her. He'd made love to her just about every way a man and woman could. He was running out of time to prove it any more thoroughly—his disability leave ended Monday. "What do you suggest? That we stop seeing each other?"

They stared at the rushing river, shards of glassy sunlight glinting and stabbing the air, violent in its own way. For Zach, his shoulders tense, his whole body waiting for her to speak, it wasn't nearly violent enough. "Well?"

All she did was shrug.

Aw, Candy. He wanted to grab her in his arms and kiss that bereft look off her face. "This is no time to go soft on me," he said gruffly. "Either you're calling it off or you aren't."

"I am." She said it, but her voice was as flinty as two stones smacked together, as brittle as the dead underbrush crackling under her feet as she backed toward the truck. "I'm sorry, Zach. I didn't want it to hurt so much. I should have stopped it earlier—"

He stopped it right then, her apologies, the tears spilling down her cheeks. He kissed her quiet and held her while her shoulders trembled with sobs. "It's all right," he heard himself say, the words tumbling into her hair, his lungs aching with the need to inhale her perfume, the earthy weedy scent of the riverbank, and Candy, just Candy, the dusting of powder on her cheek, the musky scent of her shampoo, the headband she wore, a bright blue that had looked so jaunty in town.

"I'm sorry," she repeated.

"I'm not."

She gripped his waist through his jacket, balling his shirt into fistfuls of wrinkles. "I hurt you."

"You did a lot more than that. You made me live again." He wiped away a strand of hair stuck to her face by tear tracks. Maybe coming to life naturally hurt. Babies cried, didn't they? She wanted to bury herself out there on her farm, raise vegetables instead of children. He wouldn't let her.

He had an advantage. She loved him. If she'd genuinely planned to get rid of him, she wouldn't have been in his arms. Not for the first time his heart rejoiced with an achy sweetness that was tangled like the brambles by the river, dotted with thorns, mixed up with so many painful memories they had overcome together.

As if love wasn't complicated enough, there was the insistent throb below his belt, responding to her tears and the quaking of her body on a far more elemental level.

Well, that's good, too, Zach thought. He couldn't tell her he loved her, or she'd just argue with him. He could show her, though. And show her some more.

"Candy." He traced the headband back into the shadows of her hair, skimming his fingers down the back of her neck to her sweater. "Cry it out, hon."

She clenched the lapels of his cracked leather jacket until the zipper's teeth dented her hand. "I'm sorry. I don't know why I'm such a wreck."

"You're beautiful."

"Don't say that."

Okay. He'd intended showing her anyway. He nuzzled her neck. She hiccuped. He laughed.

"Kind of nice," he murmured.

A bird started singing in a thicket of trees.

"What is?" she asked. The words came minutes too late. Her lips had lost their way, taken up with kissing his, pressing to the warmth of his cheek, the hardness of his jaw.

"Not wearing a pager," he said.

That drew their attention downward. Her hands had wound around him, burrowing into his back pockets of their own accord. Familiar. Intimate. Taking it for granted he'd never deny her access. Her fingertips pressed into his muscles as they tensed and relaxed.

He'd never told her, and certainly couldn't the way things stood between them now, but nothing turned him on harder or faster than her hands in his pockets.

"You're thinking of work?" she teased, nipping the side of his neck.

He drew in a ragged breath. "Uh, I sometimes shove

my pager in my back pocket. Opposite side from my wallet. Since I'm not on the call-out list . . ."

"And since we haven't had any rain . . ." she murmured, caressing his wallet.

"It's not likely I'd need it."

He wrapped his arms around her waist and held her so tight, nothing and no one could mistake what she did to him. "Nobody can interrupt us here."

"No." She shook her head. The tears dried quickly in the cool air, making her face feel tight. And yet a lazy warmth spread through her, flickering in her veins like heat lightning on the horizon, distant but ever closer. "It's very private."

"Like what I plan to do to you."

Her heart went still. Even the birdsong ceased. "Here?"

"Or in the truck. I don't trust that house not to come down on top of us."

"I kind of like it out here."

No more was said. The ground was soft with new moss, spongy and the slightest bit damp. The effect was startling on her hot bare skin. He took her fast, a new way, as frightening and intense as anything they'd shared. As naked in its urgency as their partially bared bodies, their skewed clothes.

The knees of his jeans were soaked and stained where he knelt between her parted legs. The heel of his palm grassy green as he held his weight off her, looking down into her eyes. She didn't care that her sweater would have mud on it by the time they were through, or that the heels of her boots would be scuffed with clay and soil.

With her jeans scrunched around her ankles, Zach's legs on top of them, she couldn't lift her knees except to cradle him. That made it tight, and the ungiving ground forced them closer together.

Her heart raced with the water. Zach drove them

both without mercy, their unheeded cries startling the birds into submissive silence while he teased and took and raced her to the edge of a river that flowed deep inside her, sweeping them both under.

He held her for a long time when it was done. "Talk about your wildlife," he muttered. "Doesn't get much wilder than that."

Candy sat up slowly, picking twigs out of her hair, collecting them in her hand like memories. His joke was no more than a tender offer, a chance to mend things. Nothing had really been settled between them. She had to say good-bye.

But when she turned to speak, his fingers brushed her hair back, outlining a streak of dirt on her cheek. "You might want a washcloth. I could get a rag from the truck, dip it in the stream."

"No." The word barely fell from her lips. He had to stop being so considerate. She nodded toward the house, the afternoon sun dropping behind the sagging roof. "How did you know this place was here?"

He indicated a pole on the edge of the property, a loop of unused line curled at the crossbar. "We disconnected it years ago." He sat up as she stood and rearranged her clothes. He did the same, plucking a blade of grass to chew on. "I knew about it before that. Pa and Joey and I went hunting down this way. We did that day."

Candy sat on the creaking steps that made up the porch and hugged her knees. "Do you come back often?"

He shook his head. "I try not to."

But he'd brought her there—when it was important they talk.

Candy scanned the small wood, the babbling river, the deserted house. A peaceful place once marred by sudden violence, by fierce lovemaking. One didn't cancel out the other. Neither did time or distance.

She'd be lying to both of them if she claimed they'd forget this, or get over it soon.

Memories weren't something you erased or out-grew. They were something you carried. She stared at Zach. Maybe the test of a hero wasn't what he did or overcame, but how he coped. Tragedy had struck Zach and his family like a lightning bolt, a flash from a shotgun in an open field, and he'd responded by devoting his own life to helping others and never expecting thanks. Or love.

He was so wrong. And she loved him so much. She'd been the one who'd taught him to love again. Was it any wonder he couldn't see past her? He'd have to.

This side of the house was in shadow now. "We should go," she said.

They walked to the truck, side by side but not touching. He drove her home without another word, kissing her good night without asking for more.

"This isn't good-bye, Candy."

It should have been. The longer they put it off, the harder it would be. "Good night, Zach."

She closed the kitchen door and stood in the dark, listening. Although his truck started, it didn't leave. A country-and-western song she couldn't completely hear sounded through his rolled-up windows and her own walled-up heart. Then he was gone.

On Saturday morning Zach's truck clattered into her yard. "I thought I told you to take the day off," she griped good-naturedly. She couldn't deny the way her heart leaped at the sight of him, torn between wanting to send him away and greedily wanting to hold him one more time.

He paced over to where she stood in the open doorway of the barn, thumbs tucked in his waistband, arms akimbo, the toe of his boot digging furrows in the ground. "Well," he drawled like some old-time cowboy, "I thought I'd take you up on what we talked about."

Her heart sank like a stone. He was doing as she asked and leaving. She kept her neighborly smile firmly in place. "Oh?"

"You wanted to show me off. Here I am." He raised his arms and turned around. He looked good, his hair combed, his face shiny from a fresh shave.

"And to what do I owe this honor?"

"You forgot?"

"Fill me in."

"Prairieland's annual meeting. As a co-operative all the members are owners; this is their chance to ask questions and hear how the place is doing."

"Kind of like a stockholders' meeting." And just about as exciting, her tone implied.

"They got hotdogs and cotton candy and free hearing tests and all sorts of pointers on how to better insulate your house and conserve electricity."

"Sounds thrilling."

"You told Ma we'd be there."

"Guilt doesn't cut it, Young."

"It isn't exactly New York nightlife, but I'll be there." He turned on his heel and headed for the truck. "And half the women in town." He didn't look back. He merely started the truck and waited.

Candy threw down her gardening gloves as if they were gauntlets.

Zach leaned over and shoved open her side door. "Thought you'd change your mind," he said with a grin.

"When it comes to sheer male vanity, you and Jesse are more related than you think."

He grinned even wider. "He's a pistol, isn't he?"

"And you're a son of a gun," she muttered, clutching her handbag as they headed into town.

The annual meeting was more country fair than stockholders' meeting. Candy was a little amazed at how quickly she'd come to recognize all the faces. Side by side with Zach, she greeted a dozen families from the tornado-stricken mobile-home park and half the merchants in Thayer. She and Zach quickly got separated—Candy deep in conversation with the local pastor about her father's congregation, Zach shooting the bull with the other linemen.

When the crowd at the tables thinned, Candy wandered into a prefabricated building filled with folding chairs. A ceremony started the meeting.

". . . if it weren't for Zach Young's quick thinking, Tom Warsaw wouldn't be here today," the general manager said. "Although we don't like it anytime it happens, we all need to remember this is dangerous work. Those lines are like lightning on a string, one touch can mean the difference between life and death. Fortunately Tom Warsaw will be back at work in a few months. And Zach Young'll be here eight A.M. Monday. Am I right, Zach?"

The crowd chuckled good-naturedly as Zach nodded.

Candy's heart was in her throat. She didn't miss the way Zach squeezed Tom Warsaw's arm as he ambled up onstage to receive a plaque and a handshake. Or the way Tom Warsaw's wife stood beside him.

Candy would never stand beside Zach that way.

She scanned the applauding crowd for single women. There was no lack of proud and admiring looks for the man onstage. Suddenly something occurred to Candy that she'd never considered: Every local girl had known for years about the tragedy with Zach and his brother. And yet none of them had gotten through to him. None had ever gotten as close as she had.

For one irrational moment she resented their failures. They hadn't tried hard enough. Hadn't seen what she had. The man needed love. Could she really turn him over to women who'd already missed that?

She searched frantically for Zach but couldn't find him through the standing, cheering audience. Suddenly there he was, striding down the far aisle, stopping inches from her. He'd looked uncomfortable onstage. He looked marvelous now.

"Believe me now when I say you're a hero, Zach?"

"Does it matter?" he asked, just for her.

"It does to me."

"Then let me be *yours*." He kissed her, a long, yielding kiss for all to see. Every inch of her responded.

In the last sensible corner of her mind, Candy heard metal chairs scraping against concrete as people nudged each other and heads turned. The boom of the general manager's voice over the microphone slowed to a halt. The applause was deafening.

Zach let her go. "Will you marry me now?"

"We can't, Zach. We can't."

She couldn't undo what she was, couldn't outrun shame and despair at the unfairness of it. But she ran all the same, tearing herself out of his arms and fleeing. In front of everyone. Just as he'd said she would.

"What do we do today?" Candy rolled up her sleeves almost before crossing the threshold of Grace's kitchen.

"We've spring-cleaned every corner of the upstairs."

"Those antiques really should be appraised," Candy scolded mildly. "You want to be sure you're insured for their full value."

"Nobody out here's going to steal the same stuff

that's in their grandmother's attics and their mother's back porches."

"I know it's different than New York, but I couldn't sleep if I didn't lock my doors."

Grace shrugged, wetting a finger to paste back a strand of hair into her perfect iron-gray coif. "Never have and never will, and people all over this county know it."

"But—"

"What if somebody needs a place to sleep? One of the Milton boys coming back from a long haul, or a lineman on a bad night?"

Like a flash of lightning the image came back to her. Candy remembered her house, the storm, the rattle of the backdoor that she'd mistaken for the wind. She remembered finding Zach sleeping in his truck.

Because of that locked door she might never have met him. He might have driven off and they'd never have—

"Candy?"

She jerked out of her reverie. "Sorry."

Grace nodded but kept her own counsel. For once Candy wished the older woman wasn't so all-fired self-contained. It'd be nice if Grace just took her by the shoulders and shook her. Somebody ought to. Her brain had been functioning on automatic pilot ever since the scene at Prairieland's annual meeting.

She'd broken it off for all to see. Her cheeks flushed red as she remembered.

He'd stopped her in the parking lot—a field crammed bumper-to-bumper with cars, the lanes marked off by little orange flags and twine.

"Where are you going?" he'd demanded.

"How can we pretend in front of everybody that we're a couple? I won't have it. I love you. You got me to say it. I do. That's why we have to stop. I can't live the way I always thought I would, with a husband and a family. I have to find another way."

"Candy."

She wrenched her arm from his grasp. "You touch me like you want to make things better and you're making them hell! If you loved me, you'd just leave me alone!"

She'd read the pain in his eyes, the pleading. And finally the pride. "What do you want me to do?" he'd asked.

She'd wanted to scream, to shake him. She'd wanted to cling to him as she had on the riverbank. "Go away. Stay away. Don't call me. For heaven's sake, don't come by."

She'd never known she had it in her to be so cruel. He took it all, squaring his shoulders and letting the storm buffet them. Then he'd reached for her.

She'd jumped back. "Don't touch me," she'd said, loud enough to turn the head of the teenage boy in charge of the makeshift parking lot.

Zach hadn't intended to. He opened his outstretched hand, the truck keys dangling there. "Take 'em. I'll get a ride home."

And yet she'd just kept talking. If only she'd had some pride, if only she'd done it clean. Instead she kept picking at the wound, trying to make it okay when it would never be all right again.

"Zach, we can't play house anymore, pretending that if we love each other everything else will take care of itself. Things don't change, not your past, not my present. I'll never have children and no amount of love will cure that."

"Dammit, Candy, I told you I don't want children."

"That's what you say now."

"Are you calling me a liar?"

"It's just the idea of someday seeing you look at me with disappointment in your eyes—" Her voice choked to a halt. She crossed her arms over her breasts and stared over the cars to the fields beyond, stretching in all directions like endless days spent alone.

"I love you," she'd said at last, rising on her toes and kissing him, a salty wet kiss, her lips brushing his, tightly closed. "If you love me, you'll leave me alone."

She gripped the keys until they cut into her palm. Then she got in and started it up. Zach appeared at the passenger window. He tossed in the plaque. "Take it. I'll pick it up sometime when you're not home."

"Zach." She reached over to touch his hand. He pulled it back as if an electric shock had burned them both. "There are some things no amount of talk will change."

Maybe he knew it. For a second she thought that's what he'd been about to say. Instead he strode through the line of cars and into the milling crowd. The meeting was over.

Everything was over.

"You really think canning jars need polishing?" Grace asked, a wry cant to her smile. The older woman had finally located Candy in the cellar, completing the last project on the spring list.

Candy gripped the dust rag in her hand, wincing at her reflection in the jar of pickles she set back on the shelf. The twenty on her right were lightly filmed with dust. The ten to her left practically glittered in the light of the bare bulb. "Just thought you'd want them clean," she said.

She couldn't fool Grace. Spring cleaning was one thing. Spring obsession was something else entirely.

What do you call this perfume? he'd asked once.

Obsession, she'd replied.

"Pickles were a dollar eighty-nine last time I looked. Don't confuse 'em with the crown jewels."

Candy laughed. Grace came over to her, her steps muffled by the dirt floor. "Hon, this isn't healthy."

"What isn't?"

"Work, work, work. Did you do this in New York after your divorce?"

Not nearly enough of it, Candy knew. That was one of the reasons she'd decided to buy a farm. "I need to keep busy, Grace."

"So does he, I suppose."

"Have you heard anything?" Candy bit her tongue the minute the words escaped. "Never mind. I'm sure he's fine."

"As far as I know," Grace said, feather-dusting the remaining jars while Candy stood around feeling useless and at loose ends.

In the three weeks since the annual meeting she'd almost grown accustomed to the feeling. She'd planted every vegetable on schedule. The rains obliged exactly when needed, not too hard, not too wet. She'd inspected the furrows daily, skimming her palm over the surface of the earth to feel the tiniest shoots of life sprouting up—like the fine hairs on a man's chest.

"Grace." Her voice sounded overloud in the cellar.

"Right here."

Candy cleared her throat. "There's been something I've been meaning to ask you. Do you mind?"

"Don't know if I do, yet. Try me."

"How do you do it? Get along so well, I mean."

"For a woman, you mean."

Candy knew the pretend offense was merely a tease. "For a woman alone."

"Because I had a damned good man once. Memories are powerful things."

Candy had those. But right now the painful ones were too mixed up with the happy ones. Try as she might, she couldn't erase Zach's look from her mind when he'd handed her the keys and she'd shouted at him. *Don't touch me.* She crossed her arms tighter.

"After Henry died, I looked around me and didn't see anything I'd ever like as much," Grace continued, repeating that when Candy's attention came back to her. "Having no alternatives, a woman learns to make do."

"True," Candy said. She had no alternatives. "There's no two ways around being infertile. You can or you can't."

"I'd've bet he wanted you more than children."

"He'd change his mind. Eventually."

Grace scoffed. "You ever know that man to change his mind on anything? He'll hold on to what's important to him a long, long time."

Candy let the words sink in, all of them true. "Then why did he let me go?" Her voice held no more substance than the dust floating on the air.

"Thought you asked him to."

Exasperated, she blurted out, "That doesn't make it any easier."

"Do you love him?"

Her eyes had rings under them, and she'd lost six pounds in three weeks. "Doesn't it show?"

"Like a stripe on a skunk. I'm just saying, if you love him, you'll give some thought to what *he* wants."

"But I have! I want him to be happy."

"Is he?"

"No." It made her miserable to think of him feeling even a fraction of what she felt.

Grace clucked and snapped off the cellar light. Sunbeams showed through the storm door as she lifted it, and they climbed out.

"Wish I could say I'd helped." The older woman

handed Candy her purse at the backdoor. "I feel good and guilty getting all this work out of you."

"It helps." She gave the older woman a hug. "You're honest with me, Grace. That means a lot."

But honesty meant facing facts not changing them. Candy mulled over what to do about Zach Young as she drove into Thayer with the dozen jars of jam Grace sent to the Meals on Wheels center in the church basement.

From Pastor Alsop to the volunteer drivers everyone seemed ready to pat her hand and find her a chair. She wasn't pregnant, for heaven's sake. She wasn't grieving either.

"Maybe you're grieving because you aren't pregnant," she grumbled, heading back out. Pastor Alsop had asked her to drive by a remote farm for one last stop of the day, perhaps sensing her need to be useful, to keep on the move.

As she took the last left-hand turn on the pastor's hastily scribbled map, she slowed for the large yellow truck looming on the side of the road. She didn't need to see the Prairieland insignia on the door. She recognized the logos on the hard hats.

And the flannel shirt on the man at the top of the pole.

She cruised by.

He was fine, working, keeping busy. So how on earth could she see, from a car in motion, the tired squint on the face of a man thirty feet off the ground?

She couldn't, not logically. In fact there was no earthly reason for her to slam on her brakes and back up at forty miles an hour, screeching to a halt on the gravel shoulder as her rear tire missed sinking into the ditch.

She hated scenes. She hated the one she'd caused in the parking lot at the annual meeting. She'd probably hate herself for this one. Right now pride didn't matter. She had a man to save.

Eleven

She stood at the bottom of the pole, arms crossed, neck craning, and nodded to Jerry.

"H-h-hello," the young man said.

She worked up a smile to put him at ease. She'd never known a person to stutter on the letter *H* before. The third crewman was more cautious, retreating to rearrange equipment at the back of the truck.

Candy waited impatiently as Zach maneuvered downward, the spikes on his heels digging into the wood. His hips took the weight as he leaned back, hitching a wide belt down the far side of the pole.

"They call that a b-b-bucking b-belt," Jerry said.

"Uh-huh." Candy refolded her arms. If he didn't hurry it up she'd climb up there and yank him down herself.

He reached bottom, taking his own sweet time unhooking the belt. He bent and unstrapped the metal braces holding his spikes on. When he straightened, Jerry was there to take them, only too eager to join the other crewman at the far end of the truck. Zach handed him the hard hat too.

"You can do that with your hand?" Candy asked without preamble, indicating the pole.

Zach pursed his lips and pulled off his leather work glove, flexing the bandaged hand. "It's been three weeks, Can."

And two days, she thought instantly. "I have to talk to you."

"Go ahead." He waited, patient as one of the poles. The kind of man who held on to things: hurts, memories, people he loved.

Candy paced halfway toward her car and back, as if searching for her anger in the gravel. She'd been ready as a fuse to argue a minute ago, yet there she was, eating him up with her eyes, flinching inside to see the guarded, cautious man she'd first met.

It was so frustrating she wanted to scream. If he loved her, really loved her, he'd do as she asked and find someone else. That was reasonable, wasn't it? Couldn't make it much clearer!

But instead of making a new life on his own, he stood silent as an elm, reliable as an oak, waiting for her to make a move.

Oh, she'd talk all right. She'd talk until his ears stung.

She wheeled around and came back, jabbing at the pocket of his flannel shirt. "Don't you dare be unhappy! I won't have it. I won't hear of you moping around glaring at people on the street."

"When did I ever—"

"Yesterday, and don't you deny it! MaryEllen Krupp says good morning to you when you buy donuts for your crew, and you practically bite her head off." Her pithy retort took him aback. "Pardon my French, but if you don't get over this, pronto, I'm going to—to take you over my knee and spank you."

He laughed, setting his hands on his hips. "Name the place."

Candy was in no mood for teasing, not when she saw his smile. It looked rusty, as if he hadn't used it for weeks, as if the crinkles weren't sure where to crinkle and the corners of his mouth had to be hoisted into place. "I did *not* put myself through all this to see you unhappy, Zach Young. Snap out of it and that's final!"

Candy marched away, then whirled when she realized he was following. "And wipe that smile off your face."

She slammed her car door and rammed the lever into "drive." Gravel spit out from under the rear quarter panel, dinging against the underside of the car.

"She's sure m-m-mad," Jerry said.

"What the heck was that?" Bill Kentin asked.

Zach grinned from ear to ear as her car disappeared over a low rise. "I think she likes me."

She loved him. And that seemed to be the only thing standing in their way.

Of all the crazy, wrongheaded notions, Zach thought. But he'd let her work her way back. Sure, his pride had taken a pounding when she'd run out on him at the annual meeting, but this separation couldn't last. Wouldn't. One day he was higher than the top of a transmitting tower, the next lower than an underground trench.

Hell, spending their lives apart wouldn't give them any more children than spending their lives together. What was the problem?

The problem was, life was full of things you didn't like and couldn't undo. Candy's choice might be one of them.

Hanging around his apartment, waiting for her to call, he kicked the refrigerator shut with his knee.

Why wouldn't she let him love her for what she was? Warts and all?

"Oh, that's great, Young. Engrave that on a Valentine." He poured a flat beer down the sink.

The phone rang. He dropped the empty can in the wastebasket and counted to five. He used his bad hand to pick up the receiver—that way he didn't have to think about how the other one shook.

"Hi, Ma."

"You coming to church Sunday?"

She sounded so matter-of-fact, it caught him off guard. In the last twenty years he'd been inside a church exactly twice, for Joey's funeral and Jesse's baptism. As if the start of one life canceled out the end of another.

"Why would you ask me that, Ma? It's been years."

"It's a special occasion, we'd appreciate your coming."

Zach rubbed the back of his neck. "Such as?"

"Your father and I are getting married."

Refusing a party, Ma and Pa had decided to celebrate their fortieth anniversary by restating their marriage vows. It was a neat idea. Too bad it meant Zach had to stand at the altar rail through three choruses of the wedding march in front of half the town. He resisted the urge to run a finger around the inside of his collar.

As his mother started down the aisle the smile on his face almost concealed the pain that had hit him the minute he'd walked into the church.

The place was the same despite a hundred happy occasions and a hundred sad. Stained glass washed the white walls with splashes of pastels. The plain pews were polished by generations of pant seats, the railing by white gloves. A few flowers and two lighted candelabra filled the air with scent.

"She there yet?" his father whispered.

"Coming now."

His father stood up straighter and smoothed back his hair.

Zach swallowed a lump. To think a man would worry about his appearance for a woman who'd seen him every day of his life for the last forty years. Maybe it wasn't so strange. He would love Candy that long. "Looking good, Pa."

At Zach's cue his father stepped forward to take his mother's hand. Zach took his sister Jean's arm and ushered her to the front row.

That's when he spotted Candy. "I'll be back there," he whispered.

Jean glanced up in surprise, turning with her husband and Jesse to watch Zach march ten rows back. Ignoring the people sliding down to make room for him on the end, he stepped across them and took his seat beside Candy.

"'Mornin'," he said.

Her gaze was riveted on the front of the church.

Chin jutting, Zach opened the hymnal as the organ music swelled. Everyone rose and sang. Zach leaned over to share with her, Candy refusing with a quick shake of her head. Her smooth contralto clipped out every phrase.

"I forgot a pastor's daughter would know all these by heart," Zach whispered.

"Shh."

He liked the way her pink lips formed that sound. "Can't find a tune in a paper sack myself."

Candy reached over and deftly flipped to the proper page. "Try it now."

It didn't help. Zach went from mouthing the words to searching for them. A church was no place to unburden one's soul, not to a woman. Up front the pastor seemed to be saying it all a hundred times better.

". . . forsaking all others, for richer or for poorer, in sickness and in health . . ."

Zach watched his mother and father. When he spoke, his voice was lower than the pastor's, softer than the drone of the organ. "Notice how Ma leans on Pa?" he asked. "Doesn't matter that he's blind. Or that I killed their oldest son."

Candy's hand covered his. He gave it a squeeze and continued. "They support each other, good times and bad. We all have crosses to bear, Candy."

"Hush."

"If I don't say it now, when can I say it?"

She shook her head, causing two fat tears to run down her cheeks. "Damn you, Zach. Stop loving me." She fumbled through her purse, muffling the snap of the latch when she withdrew a tissue. "And don't you dare look at me that way."

"I get to you. You love me."

"I always cry at weddings."

"Will you cry at ours?"

She glared at him.

The organ burst into a rumbling chord as the pastor announced the blessing and Zach's parents marched down the aisle. Everyone stood, except Zach and Candy.

"I have to go," she said.

He wasn't letting go of her hand. "Did you hear me?"

"Yes."

"We all have something we have to live with. That doesn't mean we can't live together, can't work on it together. Do you love me?"

She stood, prepared to stride out of there even if it

meant leaving her hand behind—along with her heart.

"You want me to be happy? Marry me, Candy."

"No!"

Her voice reverberated in the half-empty church. Those who'd stopped for the receiving line looked back. Some smiled. Some made way for the woman rushing past them onto the sidewalk.

"Candy!" Zach raced after her, blocked by the glut of people pausing to speak to his parents.

"'Afternoon, Zach."

"'Afternoon."

Zach nodded and shook hands, his scowl firmly in place. When he finally got free, he strutted down the steps and looked both ways. No sign of her. A tsking noise got his attention.

"Which way'd she go?" he asked his sister, Jean.

"Never you mind. I suspect it wasn't a conversation you'd want to hold on the church steps anyway."

No, it wasn't. He'd been about to drag her into his arms and win her back the way he almost had on the riverbank. The underhanded, unraveling, temporary way he knew he could. "Got a better suggestion?"

To his surprise Jean didn't tease. She put an arm around him and hugged tight. "No advice at all."

He ground his teeth and tried not to crush her beside him, grateful for even that little bit of support. "What do I do, Jeannie? Some days I think it'll work out fine . . ."

"Nights are worse, aren't they?"

"I look that bad?"

"As if you worked through ten storms."

He scanned the street for a sign of Candy's car. She must have pulled out of the back parking lot. He spotted his nephew on the corner, chatting up the Mayfield girl. "Maybe I should ask Jess. He knows all there is to know about women."

Jean laughed. "He acts like it. But that's different from loving. Isn't it?"

"I wish—" He cursed. Wishing, hoping, he was a man who *did*. But what could he do? Skywrite it over her farm? Carve *I love you* into her field with a plow? What crazy fool thing could he do to prove he loved her? Waiting had only made them both crazy.

At least the brewing stormfront to the west was bound to keep him busy through one more miserable night.

Grace hadn't meant it, Candy assured herself as she took the last casserole out of the oven.

Candy had borrowed a recipe for ten meals she'd planned to make for shut-ins. Grace had said, "Make an extra for yourself while you're at it."

"She meant the extra food," Candy reassured herself, cleaning up the kitchen. "She didn't mean you were a shut-in too." Or did she? Grace had a way of saying exactly what she meant.

Candy switched off the radio. The dial was going to break if she flipped off one more heartbreak song. Besides, the approaching storm made for nothing but static.

She pulled back the curtain by the kitchen table and peered at the band of horizon between the barn and the most decrepit of the outbuildings. Pitch-black sky and roiling clouds promised an unsettling night.

While she prepared to batten down the hatches Zach would be preparing to go out. Part of her secretly relished the idea that he was watching the same sky.

"Just don't let him take any silly risks," she prayed automatically, switching the radio back on in hopes of hearing a weather report.

What was she going to do with him? He'd looked so fine and strong, standing at that altar rail beside his father. She'd been proud. Knowing he couldn't be hers pierced her like a pitchfork.

Hours later that smile he'd turned her way as he'd come down the aisle haunted her. It wasn't carefree, it wasn't pleased, not the kind old acquaintances shared when they recognized you on the street. Or old lovers.

A sense of dread curled through her even now. It was a grim, determined smile. A man's-gotta-do-what-a-man's-gotta-do grimace worthy of John Wayne. Knowing, possessive. The man knew everything she was, had, could be. And couldn't be. He wanted her all the same.

"And what's wrong with that?" a tiny voice sounded inside her. "What's so wrong with being loved?" *In sickness and in health.*

The words mingled in the charged air. She hadn't considered the possibility of someone loving her no matter what. Jeff certainly hadn't. He'd given her every opportunity to live up to his idea—no *their* idea—of a perfect marriage.

"Yes you," she said aloud. It took two to break up a marriage; she was the one who'd offered the divorce. That he also happened to be a two-timing snake only clouded the issue. Because she couldn't be perfect, she somehow had the idea she couldn't be loved.

A bang startled her, almost as loud and clear as the pieces falling into place. She loved him. And if he was fool enough to love her, imperfections and all, she'd hang on to him for dear life.

She heard another knock, this time from the front door. She practically ran to him. There was nothing there but the shutter slamming the side of the house. She latched it and went inside to prepare for the storm. If she was going to love a lineman, she'd have to get used to spending stormy nights alone.

She bustled up and down stairs, setting pans under the peaks she knew would leak, bringing out the lantern, switching off anything that didn't need to be on. While she worked she got her arguments ready.

"You love him and he loves you. Anything else is just self-protection." She pulled on her bright yellow plastic raincoat. "So what if you can't have children? Does that mean you're unlovable? What's really unforgivable," she rattled on, gauging the rain as she opened the backdoor, "is that you hurt him to protect yourself."

The wind seized the hem of her raincoat as she stepped off the porch, tugging like a grumpy two-year-old. Stinging rain forced Candy to keep her head down as she picked her way over the slick muddy drive. She had things to see to before the storm hit in force, loose ends to tie up. She had a man to love—if he'd take her back. After this storm had cleared, she'd call him.

Hell, she'd bake him a pie.

She wheeled back the barn door on its rusty wheels. Inside eddies of wind whistled through the boards, stirring up thick musty air. Thunder crackled like dry wood. Swinging the lantern, the ground trembling beneath her feet at the dying of a louder boom, Candy looked around.

By the time she'd secured each door, hail rattled against the walls like buckshot. She found a stool under the workbench and sat, humming a song about houses dropping on people in Kansas.

The pelting rain brought out the barn smells, manure, metal, tractor tires, and diesel fuel. It smelled like leather, too, which made her think of Zach, his work belt, his gloves. Which made her think of his touch.

She heard another bang, this one like a car door slamming. "Gotta get those shutters fixed," she muttered, hoping they weren't doing too much damage to the house, calculating whether it was worth it to race the storm to the back porch.

She comforted herself with memories of the day Zach had stopped by after their first storm. She'd been so busy toting up the damage, she'd never seen the healing that had begun that night. It had been meant for him. Love had saved them both.

Forgiveness isn't only for the forgiven, she thought. She had so much to work out before she called Zach. She never doubted he'd wait for her, that's the kind of man he was. "One you can trust. Which you didn't."

But she had no time for recriminations. A sudden urgency gripped her. She wanted to call him now, to let him know before he went out in the storm that she'd been wrong to doubt him, wrong to do anything but love him.

"Dark in here."

She screamed and jumped off the stool. "Zach!"

He stepped into the light cast by the lantern she'd all but leaped over. "Careful with that thing," he said. "This floor's covered with trampled hay. You could burn this place down with a spark."

"How did you get here?"

"Truck."

She might have been persuaded by his one-word reply that he didn't care for conversation. Until she looked at him, really looked. Seconds earlier she'd wanted to tell him she was ready to accept his love. Now she wasn't sure he'd accept the offer.

The lantern barely flickered high enough to illuminate his face. Blue-white lightning cast him into shadow and silhouette. There was a harshness to him, an implacability. He'd do what he believed in no matter what she said.

"Why are you here?" she asked.

"Checking up on you."

"You don't have to work?"

"Not yet." He reached around to his back pocket and unclipped his pager, setting it on the work-bench. "If they need me, they can find me."

"From what I've heard, you're usually the first to call in."

"I've got other things to worry about now."

Helping people. Helping her. Was that all he'd come for? Her brave resolve wasn't quite so brave anymore. She wanted to touch him, to show him how strong he was and how much she admired him, to show him the man she loved deserved all the love that came his way, including hers. But he seemed so set, so starkly alone, she couldn't make the move.

"I'm fine," was all she said. If she'd said she needed him, he'd have helped her out. And if she said she loved him? "I'm sorry I hurt you." She stepped closer.

He froze, waiting for her hand to land on his arm. Candy decided there and then to go for broke. She touched his cheek, cradling it in her palm. "Take care of yourself tonight, you hear?"

His eyes were unreadable.

Stormy, she thought, her mouth quirking in a grin. "No risks on poles. Nothing dangerous."

"The whole damn job is dangerous."

Not nearly as much as his voice when it got rough, scraping, and raw.

Candy traced a fingertip along his jaw. "I know. You do dangerous work." She touched his lips before they could get into the old argument about heroics. "What I mean is, *I* don't want you getting hurt. Not again."

She reached for his left hand and lifted it to her lips. A thin line of bandage wrapped around the palm. She placed a kiss on either side of it. "I didn't want to hurt you, and I know I have."

The wind stole the words, eddying around their feet, dragging in smells of once-dusty, sodden earth, the sound of water running off the roof and down a drainpipe, splashing in the yard. The flag flapped against the aluminum pole, snapping and pinging, hollow as the quickening beat of her heart.

"Talk to me, Zach. Say something."

His fingers curled, the tips barely grazing her cheek before his hand fell. "Some things can't be solved by talk. You told me that."

Candy told herself to walk away, to find a darker corner and let the tears come. But pride had gotten her into this, and pride wasn't worth a hill of beans.

She looked in his eyes, her hair sweeping back over her shoulders as she raised her face. Tendrils fluttered back, chased off by a gust of wind careening around the corner of the barn and slipping in the door. "Apologies *are* talk. I owe you one."

"If you're going to tell me you're sorry again, forget it."

"I was wrong."

"Apparently so was I."

"No," she cried, backing away. *Don't say it. Don't tell me you were wrong to love me. It's the rightest thing either of us ever did.*

Candy walked over to the rough-sawn staircase that led to the loft and sat down. From there the wind blew full on her, scaring up bits of straw, occasional mists of rain landing on her cheeks, clammy and cool. Lightning cut across the yard, throwing everything into stark relief.

Zach came over and stood before her, shadows

and light, the outline of a man. Unreliable gusts of air carried the scent of him then fled.

"I'm not sorry if my loving you hurt," he said bluntly. "I plan to keep on hurting you."

Her heart skipped, his words almost drowned out by the pounding beat of the thunder. His hands closed around her arms and lifted her to him.

She didn't know if it was the rage outside or the suppressed passion inside that made for the chilled sensation in her bones, the uneasy heat of desire mixed with just a touch of fear, a healthy respect for the waywardness and fury of nature unleashed.

They'd unleashed it before, when touches, talk, fierce rain, and flickering fire led to a consummation neither had imagined possible. It was no different now. As his lips came down on hers she doubted it ever would be.

Her mouth opened beneath his. Their tongues parried, met, sought in the desperate darkness. When she came up for air, there was none left.

"Zach, I have to tell you."

"I love you."

"I love you."

He cupped her head in his hands and lifted her against him, setting her feet on the first rough step, his hands burrowing up under her sweater and playing across her back. "There are no words for this."

"There are. I'm sorry. I was wrong. I was protecting myself and pretending I was sparing *you*."

"Sparing me this?" He rubbed the tension out of her back until she slumped against him like a sapling bending in the wind. He peppered her neck with kisses until another tension coiled so tight in her, she wanted to cry out with it.

"I can't have children. Never, it's a fact of life. I can't be the kind of woman I want you to have."

He spit out a curse that the thunder swallowed. "Do you think I care about that? Well, I do."

Ready for denials, that hit her full force. Her knees turned watery, her lungs shallow. "You said you didn't care."

He gripped her arms, ignoring the fact that she bruised way too easy. "I care because it seems to make a hell of a lot of difference to you. And you're what matters to me. Got that? You."

Furious, he paced into the far corner of the room, stalking around the tractor, running his hands through his hair as if he could scare up the words by the roots. "When I think of what my life would've been if you hadn't come along— You're it, Candy. You made all the difference. You're the difference between what I had—which was nothing—and what I want. Which is you. Forever. Me and you, like it or not, till the end of time. And if that sounds like some worthless country song, so be it."

He waved his hand at the darkness and the thunder obliged with a roar.

Candy found herself reaching for the banister, her fingers pressing into the wood.

Zach waited for the rumble to die away, his voice as weary as the wind flailing outside, seizing what admittance it could. He stood before her, hands at his sides, his palms turned up. "Candy, I'm no good with words. I'd show you, but I've showed you and showed you—" He gave up, his final words a husky rasp. "And no matter how much I love you, you don't seem to get it."

She choked back a sob and ran to him. "Zach Young, don't you ever give up on me." She gripped his shirtfront until a button popped. It pinged off her plastic coat, but where it landed, they'd never know. "Not another word. I've said enough, I've said too much, I've said wrong things and right things. But

I've never done anything but love you from day one.
Except one thing—"

"What?"

"I let you do all the demonstrating around here."

She pulled him to her and kissed him. Not an easy
move, in fact, downright clumsy. The man was a full
head taller and that stubborn neck of his wouldn't
bend. She took his hand, remembered the bandage,
and put a handcuff grip on his wrist, leading him out
of the circle of lantern light to the bottom of the
stairs. She stepped up two steps, turned, and threw
herself so hard into his arms, she almost knocked
them down.

Almost. Zach would catch her every time. Because
he had this cockamamie idea that's how a man
showed his love for a woman, by supporting her, by
looking after her. It was her turn to say, to illustrate,
establish, insist, that a woman could do the exact
same things for her man. Talking was describing.
Loving was doing.

"Come here, you."

Twelve

The loft was damp and musty. The air scared up around them was dry and itchy and as old as the seasons.

"Candy."

"No, sir. No names."

"Is this some fantasy of yours?"

She shook her head, stopping on the top landing, edging away from the railing, promptly forgetting where they were as she concentrated solely on letting her lips convey the idea that she loved him.

She unsnapped the snaps on his flannel shirt. Her hands splayed over the warmth of his skin, a heartbeat dear as her own. "We didn't need names that first night. No fancy introductions."

"No long discussions."

"Just us. You needed me."

"I still do."

"Why did we let it get so complicated?"

"Don't ask me," he said, his voice rustling like the straw, hands firm and hard, working on the top button of her jeans. "Candy?"

"Yes?"

"I have to tell you something."

"Yes?"

"I hate this plastic."

The raincoat was gone.

"Anything else?"

"Sheesh, if it's that easy, I'm not real fond of the blouse."

She lost that too. He held her as she shrugged out of it, steadying her close to a railing that was lost in the darkness. Her breasts stroked his chest through delicate cobwebs of lace. His voice sighed like the wind in the rafters. "You always wriggle like that when you get undressed?"

"You haven't noticed?"

"I usually watch."

True, Candy thought. He liked the lights on, watching her with a mixture of desire and reverence, as if he couldn't believe his luck.

She kissed him for that.

In the dark his lips were hot, wet, ready, his tongue a bewitching prod that startled and seduced her, parting her lips with a candid sexuality that only two lovers could silently speak of.

Outside the rain drove against the walls, relentless, harsh. Inside their bodies met, fevered, partially clothed. As he laid her down prickling straw sent needles of sensation across her skin, sharp, quick, insistent. The heat inside her spread like lantern light, glowing, molten, wavering then steady as an upright flame.

She wanted more than his heat, his scent. "What do *you* want?"

"Touch me," she heard him whisper.

Feeling her way in the dark, she discovered the way sensations intensified when reduced to sounds and sighs and motions. She lifted his bad hand and gently ran the bandage over her bared breast. "I like that," she murmured, her breath a warm gust beside his ear that made him tremble.

He cupped his hand around her, the movement no longer painful. She sensed no tension in his neck or the clench of his jaw. All her tension melted, shimmering and dissolving at the stroke of his palm, his fingers trailing across the peak of her nipple.

A tongue of flame wavered through her, down and in, and she moved for him. "Zach, I love you."

He said it with his body. Two arms, pulling her closer yet. Two legs sturdy enough to part her, spread her. A waist lean enough to invite her to wrap her legs around it. A body that said "Lie with me."

He fluffed her a pillow of straw, a bed of hay. Something small scurried in a corner.

"What was that?" she asked, twisting under him.

"Scared?"

She shook her head, nuzzling her nose against his neck to let him feel the motion in the dark. "Not anymore."

"Don't go tossing your head, you might poke out an eye."

"Yes, sir," she demurred, "but that's not easy."

He teased her, strummed her skin until she mewed and wrestled, kissing her until his lips glistened with her moistness, then kissing her some more.

She writhed, and the straw whispered, the rain drumming like a pulse. The time for tenderness was over. She called his name, but the night drowned out words and demanded action.

He uncurled her hand from where she touched him wantonly, nakedly. One kiss, one whispered promise, and he drove into her, concentrating, listening, throbbing, and sure. For a moment he let the fury of passion urge them on. It didn't need children to be real, not her love, not his. For even that began with a man and a woman, and lasted, if you were lucky, long after the children were grown and gone.

He had every intention of making love with Candy for another forty years. And if he had the self-control of a monk, for another fifteen minutes.

That was before lightning illuminated her parted lips, her eyelids fluttering shut. Before thunder cracked with such force, the entire barn vibrated and trembled around them. Her body tightened around his and the subsiding flickers of lightning showed him her smile.

"Please, Zach."

She was his this night, for the first time and the last. This night they made it complete, she gave him everything. He withdrew to his tip and paused, his body rebelling at the effort.

"No, please," she begged, wrapping her arms around his neck and lifting her mouth to his ear. She licked his earlobe. His arm almost gave way.

"Hon, I've gotta hold myself off, or I'll crush you. It'll be too much."

"I want too much. I want it all, Zach."

How could a man resist? He lay full on her, her breasts cushions, her ribs like delicate bamboo. "Candy—"

"No." Her head rustled on the straw as she shook it. "Stay here. In me."

The storm receded.

"Five," she murmured, her cheek resting on his chest, the plastic raincoat sticking to her bare hip.

"I hope that's not how many times you plan on doing this tonight," he said.

She laughed and picked up a straw to tickle him. She drew it lazily across his nipple, provoking a spasm of reaction. "I was counting the time between the lightning and the thunder," she scolded.

The storm was moving off. "A minute ago it was simultaneous."

They'd exploded in ecstasy in time with the crack of thunder, lightning ripping the sky apart above them. In each other's arms they'd barely noticed, fireworks of their own rending the loft with startled cries.

"I love you," she said.

"I love you."

Simple, direct. Kind of like Zach, Candy thought, seeking his mouth. "I never thought I'd deserve someone like you. I thought by coming to Kansas I was dealing with it. Instead I ran away."

"And right into my arms. Lucky you."

Now that he'd retrieved the lantern and set it on the top stair, she could see the smug smile on his face. "You're mighty pleased with yourself."

"Pleased isn't the word."

"Happy?"

He shook his head. Her heart tripped.

"Happy isn't the word either." He palmed a handful of her rear end and squeezed. "Some things words can't do."

"But you can."

"With you. Candy."

"Yes?"

He took that darn straw out of her hand to stop her daintily drawing it up his body and tossed it in a pile of hay. "I want it to always be like this."

She laughed. "I don't know if the weatherman is willing. And think what all these storms would do to the crops!"

He could have dealt with her teasing if her hands, her whole body, hadn't been driving him to distraction. "Would you stop squirming and listen?"

"Yes?"

"I don't know when I started loving you."

She stopped his lips with love-scented fingers. "I won't insist you loved me at first sight, not even after what we did the first night. I'll accept you love me now."

"And you love me."

"I thought I didn't deserve love except on my terms."

"Meaning children."

"Mm-hmm. So I was going to outsmart life, refuse to play if I couldn't win."

His mouth, soft and giving, stopped her litany. "Enough of that." He drew her onto his body. "I love all of you. What you are, what you taste like. We can't have kids, we won't. But I'll love you every day of my life as long as I live, Candy. And that's a promise."

"In sickness and in health? Till death do us part?"

"No," he said flatly.

She planted her elbows on his chest and peered down at him. "What was that?"

"If Death himself tried to take you from me, he'd have one heck of a fight on his hands."

When he next spoke her name, it came out rusty as an old hinge.

"What?" she asked breathlessly, knowing they'd love again. In storms, in calm sultry nights. In light and darkness. In beds and other out-of-the-way places. Always in each other's arms and in each other's hearts. "What?"

He ran a hand across her hair. "If you don't stop doing that—"

"This?" She stroked him, sliding down his body to press light kisses on the way. Around him, along him, touching his thighs with tiny breaths, feather-light touches. His body quivered and shuddered until she finished. She rested her cheek against his abdomen.

After a quiet moment he tugged her hair. "Come here."

She tiptoed her way up his body with her finger-tips.

"Kiss me, Candy." She did. "Now open your mouth."

A thorough, hide-nothing, share-everything kiss followed, interrupted by the distant, pipsqueak beep of the pager going off.

"Can I use your phone?"

Candy said nothing for a stunned moment, then burst out laughing. "Zachary Young! I give you every last thing a woman can give, and you have to *ask* if I'd let you use my phone?"

"Don't get all riled now, just being polite."

"I wouldn't call anything you do after dark polite."

He grinned and searched through the straw for one of his boots. "If I'm lucky, I'll be back before dawn and we can test that theory." He touched her cheek. "Better come with me. Don't want you tripping on these stairs."

Her loving, protective man. Candy felt her eyes mist up, and her stubborn pride kick in. "I swear I don't know how I lived this long without you looking after me."

"It'll be a lot longer with me," he said. "That's a promise too."

She kissed him at the foot of the stairs. "Race you to the house."

It would be dangerous, Candy knew, him climbing poles on a night like this, assessing damage in the dark. But he'd be helping people, and that came as naturally to Zach as breathing. As naturally as him loving her, she thought with a smile. She waved him down the drive, then went back into the kitchen, setting the lantern in the window for when he came home.

Epilogue

It wasn't the old kind of tired. After two years of marriage Candy recognized when Zach had had a tough day. That old weary-of-life look he'd had when she first met him had long since left him, dissolving in a smile every time he came in the kitchen door, in the way he held her to him, kissed her, sniffed her hair and the air in general before he said, "What's for dinner?"

This day he didn't follow his usual routine.

Their second anniversary the previous week had been a private affair in front of the fireplace. Better at showing than telling, Zach had loved her with a tenderness and attention that made her heart swell even now—the memory was so recent and so sweet.

But it was Saturday, not a workday. Zach's weariness and frustration had nothing to do with a day on the job. Passing through the kitchen without a word, he sank onto the sofa. He unlaced his boots and yanked them off, leaning back and running a hand over his face.

Candy sat beside him, following that same trail

with her fingertips, coaxing a tired smile from him. "What did Jesse say?"

"He won't marry her."

"He doesn't love her?"

"He doesn't care." Zach shook his head in disgust. "I knew that boy'd get some girl pregnant one of these days. I've talked to him and talked to him. Consequences, I said. I've told him there's a world of difference between sex and love."

Zach lurched forward, elbows on his knees, and absently rubbed the palm of his left hand with his right. Candy covered both hands with hers. "Let me do it." Carefully kneading the area around the old scar, she watched him flex a finger at a time. "Somehow it's not surprising, not with Jesse. And it isn't your fault."

"No, it's just that when you love a woman, you . . ." His voice faltered to a stop as he looked into Candy's eyes. "Speaking of which, why am I complaining?" He wrapped his free arm around her neck and tugged her gently to him. "It's good to be home."

Two years hadn't dimmed what he could do to her. If anything, knowing the heights his touch could take her to only intensified her reaction. She opened for him, took his tongue in her mouth, loved him in a tantalizing imitation of the act itself.

"A damn shame," Zach murmured, his breathing harsh as he pulled away from her.

"What is?"

"That something so beautiful can be used for sport."

"Not every man is as good as you."

"You can say that again."

She laughed at his leer, but the smiles faded when he kissed her again. Less a sharing than a promise of things to come, it was an erotically charged demonstration, an intimacy found only in the dark.

He was all the husband any woman would wish, Candy thought.

Ten minutes after meeting Zach her father had said, "You've got a good man there," just as she'd predicted. He would've said it sooner but chose to wait for Zach to unload the baggage in the truck.

Not only a good man, she thought, he'd make a great father too.

Suddenly Candy hugged Zach hard.

"What's this?" he asked, laughing as they fell back on the sofa. He steadied her on his chest.

"I just wish every woman in the world was as lucky as I am."

"I'd be an exhausted man."

She pinched him playfully. "Don't be egotistical, you sound like Jesse. I just meant, it's so sad about Karen. Not having a man to love her."

"Yeah." His face grew serious. "Just ready to go off to college, and Jesse has to come along and sweet-talk her. Everybody's surprised. She had such a good head on her shoulders, always mature, goal setting."

"The promise of love can be very seductive."

"When it's real." He touched his lips to hers again, his hand hungrily cupping her breast, possessively stroking her body.

Candy quivered.

Zach smiled, his eyes darkening. "If there's nothing on the stove, maybe we could continue this in the bedroom."

Candy pulled herself together. She had something she wanted to talk about first. The bedroom would be a good place to discuss it, but they had a tendency to forget all about words once they were there. "I—I wanted to talk about Karen more."

Zach looked surprised, then understanding dawned and he sat up beside her, taking her hands in both of his. "It must be tough for you, seeing someone else having a baby she's not even sure she wants when you'd be such a great mother. It's all right with me, Candy. You know that." He put an arm around her and tucked her cheek into his shoulder. "I just wish it was easier for you."

Drat her cowardly soul, but Candy was grateful he couldn't see her face. "So you know she doesn't want the baby."

"I gather she'd love to have it but isn't in any real position to raise it. At least that's the impression I got in the hour-long lecture I just gave Jesse. When he could get a word in edgewise, that is. Of course he's not the most reliable judge."

"She's planning to give it up for adoption."

"Yeah?"

"If she can find the right family. She told me."

"When?"

Candy hesitated. Until then it had been so much conversation. But as she paused Zach's breathing changed, his heart sped up as she laid her hand over it. She looked up at him and spoke softly—it was the only way she could keep her voice steady. "She came over. She knew you were going to talk to Jesse, and she wanted to talk to me."

Zach cautiously combed her hair back off her face, holding it there, his fingers just grazing her ear. "She was here?"

Candy nodded, seeking the warmth of his palm near her cheek. She'd never forget he was touching her when she told him, or his look of quiet astonishment. "She asked me if we wanted to adopt, Zach. She doesn't want her baby going to strangers. She'd like to know it was raised here, in her hometown, by people who'd love very much to have a baby."

Zach looked away a minute. Even after two years there were times Candy couldn't decipher every look,

times when he retreated to deal with his own de-
mons. But he always came back to her. "Can."

"Yes?" She bit her lip.

Zach almost groaned. He'd do anything for her
when she bit her lip and looked up at him the way
she was. The woman ran the farm as if she'd come
from a generation of farmers. She handled the ship-
ping and the bills, she whipped up meals for every
charity thing in town, and she wrapped him around
her little finger as easily as a ten-year-old knots his
shoelaces. He'd just never thought, in the mess he'd
made of his life up until now, that it'd be *his* ten-
year-old someday. *Theirs.*

Or that it was possible to love a woman as much as
he loved Candy.

"You want this baby, Candy?"

She nodded. The motion made tears roll down her
cheeks in two fat drops.

"That's all I need to know," he almost said. But
before the words could get out, his throat closed up,
and his mouth refused to move except for a crooked
grin on one corner. He nodded hard and managed a
grunt. "Okay."

Candy threw her arms around his neck. "I knew
it!"

"You knew we'd have a baby? I thought you'd given
up on that."

No, she thought, laughing and sobbing and wiping
away tears with her sleeve. Candy had known from
the moment Zach had walked in the door that when
she told him Karen's proposal, he would answer her
honestly and firmly in one word or less. Her man
didn't go in for long debates. He knew what was
important, and he held on to what he loved.

If they discussed the pros and cons of open adoption, it would be later, in bed or over breakfast,
sitting at the table and glancing out over the fields,

their hands touching and holding for long moments as their gazes met. Daily life would grind to a halt and time would slow down just enough to let them know they were home, they had each other.

"I love you, Zach."

"I love you."

"Do you want a boy or girl?"

"That's up to Karen, isn't it? And that wastrel nephew of mine."

"He can stop by."

"At least he'll know his child somewhat. Maybe he'll see what he's missing, what really matters in life."

"Having someone to love," Candy murmured.

"The real thing, not those one-night imitations of his."

Candy looked at the man she loved. "The kind of love that lasts a lifetime."

"Longer." He held her hard. "This is for you, Candy. Your baby. If Karen hadn't seen what a good woman you are, she wouldn't have asked you."

"And what a great man I married. Have I told you how lucky I was to find you?"

"About ten times since our anniversary."

"You didn't give up on me."

"We'd both given up on ourselves, I think."

"Giving to others and never expecting anything for ourselves."

He laughed suddenly and squeezed her to him. "Well, hon, we're expecting now."

Her laughter floated behind them all the way into the bedroom, stopping on a sigh only when Zach laid her down, covering her body with his.

"I'll never make that mistake again," he said. "Loving you saved my life."

"And mine. I love you, Zach."

"I love you. Let me prove it."

He already had, Candy thought as his fingers twined with hers to undo the buttons of her blouse, as his lips skimmed her cheek, her temple. He had proved his love in a hundred ways, and as long as they lived, he'd go on proving it. And she would never, ever stop believing him.

THE EDITOR'S CORNER

There's a lot to look forward to from LOVESWEPT in October—five fabulous stories from your favorites, and a delightful novel from an exciting new author. You know you can always rely on LOVESWEPT to provide six top-notch—and thrilling—romances each and every month.

Leading the lineup is Marcia Evanick, with **SWEET TEMPTATION,** LOVESWEPT #570. And sweet temptation is just what Augusta Bodine is, as Garrison Fisher soon finds out. Paleontologist Garrison thinks the Georgia peach can't survive roughing it in his dusty dinosaur-fossil dig—but she meets his skepticism with bewitching stubbornness and a wildfire taste for adventure that he quickly longs to explore . . . and satisfy. Marcia is at her best with this heartwarming and funny romance.

Strange occurrences and the magic of love are waiting for you on board the **SCARLET BUTTERFLY,** LOVESWEPT #571, by Sandra Chastain. Ever since Sean Rogan restored the ancient—and possibly haunted—ship, he'd been prepared for anything, except the woman he finds sleeping in his bunk! The rogue sea captain warns Carolina Evans that he's no safe haven in a storm, but she's intent on fulfilling a promise made long ago, a promise of love. Boldly imaginative, richly emotional, **SCARLET BUTTERFLY** is a winner from Sandra.

Please give a big welcome to new author Leanne Banks and her very first LOVESWEPT, **GUARDIAN ANGEL,** #572. In this enchanting romance Talia McKenzie is caught in the impossible situation of working very closely with Trace Barringer on a charity drive. He'd starred in her teenage daydreams, but now there's bad blood between their families. What is she to do, especially when Trace wants nothing less from her than her love? The answer makes for one surefire treat. Enjoy one of our New Faces of 1992!

Ever-popular Fayrene Preston creates a blazing inferno of desire in **IN THE HEAT OF THE NIGHT**, LOVESWEPT #573. Philip Killane expects trouble when Jacey finally comes home after so many years, for he's never forgotten the night she'd branded him with her fire, the night that had nearly ruined their lives. But he isn't prepared for the fact that his stepsister is more gorgeous than ever . . . or that he wants a second chance. An utterly sensational romance, with passion at its most potent—only from Fayrene!

In Gail Douglas's new LOVESWEPT, **THE LADY IS A SCAMP**, #574, the lady in the title is event planner Victoria Chase. She's usually poised and elegant, but businessman Dan Stewart upsets her equilibrium. Maybe it's his handshake that sets her on fire, or the intense blue eyes that see right inside her soul. She should be running to the hills instead of straight into his arms. This story showcases the winning charm of Gail's writing—plus a puppet and a clown who show our hero and heroine the path to love.

We end the month with **FORBIDDEN DREAMS** by Judy Gill, LOVESWEPT #575. When Jason O'Keefe blows back into Shell Landry's life with all the force of the winter storm howling outside her isolated cabin, they become trapped together in a cocoon of pleasure. Jason needs her to expose a con artist, and he also needs her kisses. Shell wants to trust him, but so much is at stake, including the secret that had finally brought her peace. Judy will leave you breathless with the elemental force raging between these two people.

On sale this month from FANFARE are three exciting novels. In **DAWN ON A JADE SEA** Jessica Bryan, the award-winning author of **ACROSS A WINE-DARK SEA**, once more intertwines romance, fantasy, and ancient history to create an utterly spellbinding story. Set against the stunning pageantry of ancient China, **DAWN ON A JADE SEA** brings together Rhea, a merperson from an undersea world, and Red Tiger, a son of merchants who has vowed revenge against the powerful nobleman who destroyed his family.

Now's your chance to grab a copy of **BLAZE,** by bestselling author Susan Johnson, and read the novel that won the *Romantic Times* award for Best Sensual Historical Romance and a Golden Certificate from *Affaire de Coeur* "for the quality, excellence of writing, entertainment and enjoyment it gave the readers." In this sizzling novel a Boston heiress is swept into a storm of passion she's never imagined, held spellbound by an Absarokee Indian who knows every woman's desires. . . .

Anytime we publish a book by Iris Johansen, it's an event—and **LAST BRIDGE HOME** shows why. Original, emotional, and sensual, it's romantic suspense at its most compelling. It begins with Jon Sandell, a man with many secrets and one remarkable power, appearing at Elizabeth Ramsey's cottage. When he reveals that he's there to protect her from danger, Elizabeth doesn't know whether this mesmerizing stranger is friend or foe. . . .

Also on sale this month in the Doubleday hardcover edition is **LADY DEFIANT** by Suzanne Robinson, a thrilling historical romance that brings back Blade, who was introduced in **LADY GALLANT.** Now Blade is one of Queen Elizabeth's most dangerous spies, and he must romance a beauty named Oriel who holds a clue that could alter the course of history.

Happy reading!

With warmest wishes,

Nita Taublib
Associate Publisher
LOVESWEPT and FANFARE

OFFICIAL RULES TO WINNERS CLASSIC SWEEPSTAKES

No Purchase necessary. To enter the sweepstakes follow instructions found elsewhere in this offer. You can also enter the sweepstakes by hand printing your name, address, city, state and zip code on a 3" x 5" piece of paper and mailing it to: Winners Classic Sweepstakes, P.O. Box 785, Gibbstown, NJ 08027. Mail each entry separately. Sweepstakes begins 12/1/91. Entries must be received by 6/1/93. Some presentations of this sweepstakes may feature a deadline for the Early Bird prize. If the offer you receive does, then to be eligible for the Early Bird prize your entry must be received according to the Early Bird date specified. Not responsible for lost, late, damaged, misdirected, illegible or postage due mail. Mechanically reproduced entries are not eligible. All entries become property of the sponsor and will not be returned.

Prize Selection/Validations: Winners will be selected in random drawings on or about 7/30/93, by VENTURA ASSOCIATES, INC., an independent judging organization whose decisions are final. Odds of winning are determined by total number of entries received. Circulation of this sweepstakes is estimated not to exceed 200 million. Entrants need not be present to win. All prizes are guaranteed to be awarded and delivered to winners. Winners will be notified by mail and may be required to complete an affidavit of eligibility and release of liability which must be returned within 14 days of date of notification or alternate winners will be selected. Any guest of a trip winner will also be required to execute a release of liability. Any prize notification letter or any prize returned to a participating sponsor, Bantam Doubleday Dell Publishing Group, Inc., its participating divisions or subsidiaries, or VENTURA ASSOCIATES, INC. as undeliverable will be awarded to an alternate winner. Prizes are not transferable. No multiple prize winners except as may be necessary due to unavailability, in which case a prize of equal or greater value will be awarded. Prizes will be awarded approximately 90 days after the drawing. All taxes, automobile license and registration fees, if applicable, are the sole responsibility of the winners. Entry constitutes permission (except where prohibited) to use winners' names and likenesses for publicity purposes without further or other compensation.

Participation: This sweepstakes is open to residents of the United States and Canada, except for the province of Quebec. This sweepstakes is sponsored by Bantam Doubleday Dell Publishing Group, Inc. (BDD), 666 Fifth Avenue, New York, NY 10103. Versions of this sweepstakes with different graphics will be offered in conjunction with various solicitations or promotions by different subsidiaries and divisions of BDD. Employees and their families of BDD, its division, subsidiaries, advertising agencies, and VENTURA ASSOCIATES, INC., are not eligible.

Canadian residents, in order to win, must first correctly answer a time limited arithmetical skill testing question. Void in Quebec and wherever prohibited or restricted by law. Subject to all federal, state, local and provincial laws and regulations.

Prizes: The following values for prizes are determined by the manufacturers' suggested retail prices or by what these items are currently known to be selling for at the time this offer was published. Approximate retail values include handling and delivery of prizes. Estimated maximum retail value of prizes: 1 Grand Prize ($27,500 if merchandise or $25,000 Cash); 1 First Prize ($3,000); 5 Second Prizes ($400 each); 35 Third Prizes ($100 each); 1,000 Fourth Prizes ($9.00 each) ; 1 Early Bird Prize ($5,000); Total approximate maximum retail value is $50,000. Winners will have the option of selecting any prize offered at level won. Automobile winner must have a valid driver's license at the time the car is awarded. Trips are subject to space and departure availability. Certain black-out dates may apply. Travel must be completed within one year from the time the prize is awarded. Minors must be accompanied by an adult. Prizes won by minors will be awarded in the name of parent or legal guardian.

For a list of Major Prize Winners (available after 7/30/93): send a self-addressed, stamped envelope entirely separate from your entry to: Winners Classic Sweepstakes Winners, P.O. Box 825, Gibbstown, NJ 08027. Requests must be received by 6/1/93. DO NOT SEND ANY OTHER CORRESPONDENCE TO THIS P.O. BOX.

FANFARE
On Sale in August

DAWN ON A JADE SEA

☐ 29837-2 $5.50/6.50 in Canada
by Jessica Bryan

bestselling author of ACROSS A WINE-DARK SEA

She was a shimmering beauty from a kingdom of legend. A vision had brought Rhea to the glorious city of Ch'ang-an, compelling her to seek a green-eyed, auburn-haired foreign warrior called Zhao, the Red Tiger. Amid the jasmine of the Imperial Garden, passion will be born, hot as fire, strong as steel, eternal as the ocean tides.

BLAZE

☐ 29957-3 $5.50/6.50 in Canada
by Susan Johnson

bestselling author of FORBIDDEN and SINFUL

To Blaze Braddock, beautiful, pampered daughter of a millionaire, the American gold rush was a chance to flee the stifling codes of Boston society. But when Jon Hazard Black, a proud young Absarokee chief, challenged her father's land claim, Blaze was swept up in a storm of passions she had never before even imagined.

LAST BRIDGE HOME

☐ 29871-2 $4.50/5.50 in Canada
by Iris Johansen

bestselling author of THE GOLDEN BARBARIAN

Jon Sandell is a man with many secrets and one remarkable power, the ability to read a woman's mind, to touch her soul, to know her every waking desire. His vital mission is to rescue a woman unaware of the danger she is in. But who will protect her from him?